NEW WORLDS, OLD WAYS

SPECULATIVE TALES FROM THE CARIBBEAN

EDITED BY KAREN LORD

PEEKASH
PRESS

All names, characters, places, and incidents are the product of the authors' imaginations. Any resemblance to real events or persons, living or dead, is entirely coincidental.

Published by Peekash Press
©2016 Peekash Press
Foreword ©2016 Karen Lord

USA (Akashic): ISBN: 978-1-61775-526-2
UK (Peepal Tree): ISBN: 978-1-84523-336-5
Library of Congress Control Number: 2016949537

An earlier version of Richard B. Lynch's "Water Under the Bridge" first appeared in *POUi: The Cave Hill Journal of Creative Writing.*

Supported using public funding by
**ARTS COUNCIL
ENGLAND**

Peekash Press (US office)
c/o Akashic Books
Brooklyn, New York
Twitter: @AkashicBooks
Facebook: AkashicBooks
info@akashicbooks.com
www.akashicbooks.com

Peekash Press (UK office)
c/o Peepal Tree Press
17 King's Avenue, Leeds LS6 1QS, United Kingdom
Twitter: @peepaltreepress
Facebook: peepaltreepress
E-mail: contact@peepaltreepress.com
Website: www.peepaltreepress.com

Also Available from Peekash Press

PEPPERPOT
Best New Stories from the Caribbean

COMING UP HOT
Eight New Poets from the Caribbean

Table of Contents

Foreword
by Karen Lord

When Jeremy Poynting of Peepal Tree Press invited me to put together an anthology of speculative fiction, my immediate response was to decline. I thought it was a brilliant idea, but given the short time-frame and the complicated nature of Caribbean speculative fiction, I doubted I could curate a selection that would do justice to the genre.

Some writers (and readers) think that speculative fiction (an umbrella term for science fiction, fantasy, and several other subgenres of improbable what-ifs) consists of Tolkien pastiches and pulpy space opera written in mediocre prose. They overlook Caribbean icons like Edgar Mittelholzer, Erna Brodber, Jamaica Kincaid and Nalo Hopkinson (to name but a few) with their richness of folklore, myth, parable and satire. The problem is not quality, it is definitions. There is a longstanding tradition of Caribbean literature with fantastical or speculative elements in both prose and poetry. Try to find those works, however, and they are often hidden in plain sight amid the bulk of our literary canon in small presses, academic journals and region-specific imprints and publications.

The project of collecting past works remains one for a later date. *This* anthology looks to the future, to new writers and new works of Caribbean speculative fiction, by taking advantage of a fortunate set of circumstances. In 2014, the Government of Bermuda invited Grenadian-born author Tobias Buckell to lead a workshop in speculative fiction, and the organisers of the Bocas Lit Fest (Trinidad & Tobago) asked me to do the same for the Bocas South festival later that year. The Bocas Lit Fest 2015 schedule included a workshop with Nalo Hopkinson, Tobias Buckell, Trinidadian author R.S. Garcia and myself. These workshops were attended by writers of all kinds, from die-hard readers of the genre to curious novices. I am grateful to the Government of Bermuda and the organising team of the Bocas Lit Fest for their recognition of the importance of the genre in our region's literary development.

Most of the submissions to this anthology came from workshop participants. I found more potential works via the University of the West Indies (St Augustine and Cave Hill). Established editors and educators in the literary community recommended more emerging writers. I am indebted to Professor Funso Aiyejina, Lisa Allen-Agostini, Professor Jane Bryce, Tobias Buckell and Robert Edison Sandiford for their help.

However, the final selection demonstrates the limitations of the known networks. This anthology does not represent the entire region. This is only a start, and more may be achieved, perhaps in volumes yet to come. For now, in the year 2016, we are pleased to present to you *New Worlds, Old Ways: Speculative Tales from the Caribbean*.

Do not be misled by the 'speculative' in the title. Although there may be rockets and robots and fantastical creatures, these tales are not copies of worn-out tropes. The common symbols of speculative fiction are merely tools to frame the familiar. These are stories of survival—survival of the individual, the family, the community, the nation, the region, and the world or worlds that we inhabit. Survival is more than mere living. We need to relate: to connect, to identify, to tell our stories, to draw lines from past to present and from each to each, and thence as far forward as we can to the unborn generations.

Here you will find the recent past and ongoing present of government and society with curfews, crime and corruption. Here are the universal themes of family with parents and children, growth and death, love and hate. Here is the struggle to survive and thrive when power is capricious and revenge too bittersweet; and here too is the passage of everything . . . old ways, places, peoples, and ourselves . . . leaving nothing behind but memories, histories, stories.

This anthology also speaks to the fragility of home, something that is not always understood by those who inhabit countries with more resources and choices. Unmitigated dystopia in fiction may be enjoyed by those who live securely, but this region suffers under crises of economy and climate and a history shadowed with genocide. I am wary and weary of literature that depicts the utter extinction, physical or cultural, of a people who still fight to survive. Fortunately, this anthology reminds the reader that although home may be vulnerable, it is also beautifully resilient. The voice of our literature declares that in spite of disasters, this people and this place shall not be wholly destroyed.

I am grateful for the opportunity to work on this anthology. These new stories have shown me that our horizons continue to be wider than our borders, and that our literature does not only entertain—it transforms. Read for delight, then read for depth, and you will not be disappointed.

I look forward to the future works that these authors will produce, and the future worlds that their work will inspire.

TAMMI BROWNE-BANNISTER

Once in a Blood Moon
Barbados

S he threw her piss in the yard of a Nightingale House, in the
Republic, on the east of the island. Her name was Gaiutra
and she had no one.

She dreamt she had fallen out of a coconut tree. That wasn't
hard for her to imagine. She grew a thick reddish-brown husk on
her scalp and fine bristles ran down her arms and legs. Every day,
the children teased her about falling out of a coconut tree until
she saw such an image in her sleep. What else was she supposed
to think, anyhow? Her birth was mysterious. Her parents were
figments that never came to claim her. All those years–the moon
moved in front of the sun and as a shadow grew over the earth,
people got dim, dimmer and darker. Secretive and superstitious.
Gaiutra didn't know that on the night she was born the earth
had passed between the moon and the sun. It was the first in a
series of lunar eclipses that would determine her fate forever.

Those blasted children at the home were wicked and nasty.
They called her leatherback. Said she smelled like the Careen-
age in Bridgetown, during low tide. Their hands came down on
her back like hammers. Their fingernails tattooed her olive flesh
until scaly patterns stitched themselves into place. No, Gaiutra
didn't stand there, take all the blows. She slapped them for 1, not

knowing her parents; 2, not knowing her date of birth; 3, saying she fell out of a coconut tree; and 4, because she believed them when they said she rolled into the stony yard of this restored Victorian house with a hard-to-spell-and-hard-to-break-down-into-syllables-name like Gaiutra.

She never cried for owning an exaggerated beak on her face—for the oversized head on her neck—for tough skin and a broad back—for being different. Each New Year came and she lit a candle for being extraordinary. That was how she had chosen to celebrate her life on land.

One day, an old woman who worked at the home as a cleaner noticed how Gaiutra had been spending her days. Disengaged. Alone. In isolation. Sitting on a ledge of the veranda that overlooked Shell Bay, staring at the ocean's undulating waves.

"What you doing here by yourself?" the woman said to her.

"Catching fish with my eyes," Gaiutra said, keeping her gaze set on the sea ahead of them.

"What kinda fish do you see?"

"Flying fish," she said, as a smile beamed across her face.

"How you so sure that's what you see?"

Gaiutra's shoulders went up and down. As the woman came closer, the girl smelled sunshine and sea breeze. "I can't explain, but for some reason I can see very far, very well. I can see the fish skittering on the surface of the water. I can hear the droplets, like heartbeats, falling back into the ocean. I can smell those creatures, too, Auntie," she said to the old woman, who nodded as if she knew for sure that this was so.

"I know a story about the sun and moon, the stars, the sea and shells and gorgeous creatures like the dorado. I know a ton of stories. You want to hear them?' the woman said with an expectant look on her face. Gaiutra nodded.

The old woman, whom all the children at Nightingale House called Auntie, went on to tell of the time when she appeared from the indigenous hat shell. Gaiutra grew to love this woman and her fantastic stories. She called her Auntie Cowrie because her smile reminded Gaiutra of a cowrie shell with a jagged gap in its middle. Through this woman, Gaiutra learned of the awesome powers of Poseidon, the god of the sea. From this day, there grew a tug of excitement in her belly, which became stronger and stronger, whenever she heard a new story.

Years later, after two more lunar eclipses, Gaiutra blossomed into a beautiful young woman. She still struck a match when the moon was full, cold and giddy blue. She danced on the warm sands of Foul Bay, below the shedding mile trees, not too far from the chattel house that she rented, after her emancipation from Nightingale House. She had found work with a local conservation agency, recording the variety of shells, saving coral reefs and sea life.

Two weeks before the arrival of an auspicious moon, her Auntie Cowrie passed away. With no family of her own, Gaiutra took it upon herself to bury the woman. Gaiutra laid her Auntie Cowrie on a bed of periwinkles and shells in a cemetery not far from her home. She placed a wreath made of purple and yellow sea fans on top of the grave. She cried for the first time in ages.

That night, in her sleep, she saw the woman's kind but craggy face—rough top, salty curls, and a sprinkling of poppy seeds that dotted her cheeks—that cowrie shell smile. "Dead people will not rest unless they can tell one last story," Gaiutra said to herself when she received such a blessing from her auntie:

"Many phases ago, your Mother used to follow the moon. She would come ashore and drop her eggs in the sands of Foul Bay. Her natal beach. Your natal home. Good people saved your siblings. Bad people boiled them for food. Your Mother didn't make the journey alone. She returned with a few of her own sisters. Some were captured, became delicacies for the highest bidder, their shells sold as wall ornaments.

"Once upon a time, your ancestors had to make such an arduous journey and if people were around, they would have to abandon their plan to drop their descendants on land. Before Poseidon, Man and the Goodnight Moon, they dropped their eggs into the sea and swam back home—exhausted and hungry but free.

"I was told a story of those who journeyed to Trinidad to lay eggs on the packed shores of Matura. The local conservationists rescued the eggs and hatchlings from poachers, mongooses, the wretched corbeaux, from people who supported the circle of life and had given it new meaning by catching newborns to feed land crabs and pigs. Grande Riviere had become feeding ground. The corbeaux circled like vultures. They waited for the hatchlings to emerge. When they did, half-cracked shells and carcasses without heads were strewn across the sandy ground. The beach reeked of sulphur and death. Only a few escaped into the sea.

Years ago, I heard a grisly story of what had happened to unfortunate hatchlings in Speightstown. The saying goes: plantain suckers follow the root. Well, before there was a road that cut into Speightstown, just by the new hotel, all there was beach land. When the turtles returned, they crossed over the embankment from the sea onto the paved road to the exact spot in which they had nested. Weeks later, when the hatchlings burst through the sand, they saw what appeared to be moonlight. The hatchlings followed the bright glow out of the sandy banks, past the tall cane grasses, toppled over the sidewalk onto the asphalt. They were scattered about the road in confusion. The yellow light led them everywhere except towards the sea. They didn't know it was a streetlight that fed them into oncoming traffic. It wasn't difficult for Man to disregard a life whether belonging to a mere turtle or one of their own species.

"When the hatchlings were killed, Poseidon became furious. He flushed the earth with the sea. He purged the world until the lives taken equalled those pummelled into the asphalt and those hunted and killed. Then he caused a miracle to happen for a few of his creatures.

"Every time there was a blood moon, a few of the hatchlings became human beings, but always inclined to the sea and light. On their thirtieth anniversary, they would become their true form again. To make this transition, they had to give birth. I found you many, many moons ago. You are one of Poseidon's specially chosen daughters, and soon you will take on your true form when the earth casts a shadow upon a super moon."

Gaiutra loved what she had heard. She liked the part about not falling haphazardly like a nut from a tree. Everything was now majestic and beautiful to her eyes and ears. She would never question her existence again. The god of humans didn't like it when anyone questioned his work. She was sure her own god had his own feelings about anyone who challenged him.

It was her Auntie Cowrie's stories that spurred her into working as a conservationist. Gaiutra recalled her first time rescuing the hatchlings from predators. Oncoming traffic posed threats to life. No matter how much she flailed her arms to flag down a speeding vehicle, the traffic mashed the turtles into the asphalt. Water came to her eyes as she recorded the number of deaths. "This is a sign of the times," she said to herself. Whilst she couldn't blame drivers for trying to knock down someone they perceived as a deranged criminal, why couldn't they make out the tiny creatures crawling around to find the sea. Gaiutra had rescued many turtles from artificial light in and around the island and taken them to darker beaches as their nesting places.

She sat on the beach, chewing on seaweed snacks and drinking a fizzy Plus. She had Foul Bay to herself because of the Blood

Moon Bash at St. Lawrence Gap. She glided a hand over her tummy as she recalled her decision to jump for Crop Over that summer.

It was on impulse when after one mas camp spoke to her with their *Under the Sea* theme, she jumped with the loggerheads section in the broiling sun that turned her skin to a dry green-ish-brown tone. When her troupe got to Spring Garden, Gaiutra had an irresistible urge to take a sea bath. She walked into the Caribbean-blue waters. The waves folded themselves over one another until there was foam. Gaiutra felt calmed, the sea warm.

Her first and only sexual experience was unlike anything she had ever read in magazines, or seen on television. She felt a series of tickles up and down her thighs, like those felt when swimming through slippery sargassum. Whatever it was latched itself onto her body and slipped into the space between her legs. Her toes curled. Her body quivered and a pleasurable feeling surged through her. When the sensation was over, Gaiutra dipped her head under the water only to glimpse an albino hawksbill turtle swimming away. A rare sighting: that species of turtle had a short lifespan.

Now sitting upon sandstone, in moonlight, Gaiutra made light of her situation. If an old person was around, she would be told that sitting on hard, cold surfaces could give her a cold, varicose veins, piles, and a bladder infection. If that person knew of the child she carried, they would say it could cause the child to be stillborn. Gaiutra felt the wriggling movements of her unborn inside her womb.

The truth was Gaiutra had become tired of all the moon and sea stories that she told herself. "Enough now, nuh. A moon is just a moon." For that reason, she played mas–to escape herself, do something normal for a change. Now, awaiting the blood moon's arrival, Gaiutra realised how impatient she had been–that this restlessness and rebellion only propelled her closer to her fate. She found comfort in staring at the moon and listening to the lapping sounds of the sea.

Earlier in the evening, she had taken photographs of the super moon. It was a perfect circle and the brightest of flood-lights she had ever seen. There was a spotlight on the water and a long shimmering shadow streaked the ocean. She put the camera down, satisfied with the shots she had taken. She dug her feet into the warm sand, feeling the grains escaping through the spaces between her toes. She dug some more. The hole got large enough to roast breadfruits. She continued digging. Soon the hole was big enough, but for what? Gaiutra didn't know and she didn't wonder about it for long. The super moon kept rising higher and higher into the steely blue sky. Hours later, a shadow crept across its face.

She pulled a tripod from her bag and set it up in a clearing of sand, stones and shells. She placed the camera on the tripod. A shadow stretched across the moon until its brilliance gradually faded. Gaiutra changed lenses. Her camera hummed as she took more pictures.

The shadow swallowed the landscape of the moon until it began to bleed.

Water as warm as the sand gushed down Gaiutra's legs. Sprinkled her toes. She began to pack up her things. Pain struck through her spine, ripped through her belly down to her legs. She fell to her knees, began to bear down. She eased her under-wear off. Pain struck through her again. She lay still on her side. Her breathing grew heavy. She crawled until she got to the hole in the sand. She crouched over it and bore down when the pain clawed at her womb. She pushed down harder and longer. *Breathe in. Breathe out,* like the women she saw in the videos. She bore down until there was crowning. Rested.

The stiffness in her belly returned. Gaiutra pushed harder and longer until she delivered a large sack into the sand. She lay down on her side and peered into the hole. She ran a hand over the silky attachment that covered her newborn, and she became frightened. Gaiutra had heard of humans who expelled their shame into plastic bags, discarding them on the bay. *Was this the way?* Her eyes widened with fear.

The sharp stitches subsided. Instinct guided her mind. She glided close to the hole and used her hands and feet to sweep the sand, packing it down over the opening until the thing was covered. Gaiutra rested for a few minutes. The last bit of light filtered from the moon onto the land. The wind picked up. It filled the air with those hairy leaves from the mile trees. Soon, a figure rose out of the sand until it was shrouded in foliage. Gaiutra looked on in fascination. She imagined this was how her auntie had come into existence. The presence walked over to where Gaiutra lay on the ground and placed a hand against her face. It was then that Gaiutra realised this was her Auntie Cowrie.

"You're back," she said to the woman.

"Yes. Because of your sacrifice, I am needed again."

"I'm glad."

Gaiutra crawled into the cool waters. She dipped her head below the surface of the Atlantic Ocean. When she emerged, a gilded carapace clung to her back and fins propelled her further out from shore. She looked back at Foul Bay and saw her Auntie Cowrie excavating the nest where she had delivered her newborn. She could see the sand blowing around in the wind. The digging stopped and Gaiutra guessed her Auntie Cowrie had uncovered the caul. She smiled at this. Gaiutra gazed into the sky. The last light vanished; the super moon was now bludgeoned red. She glanced at the bay one last time, dipped her head into the sea, and swam away.

SUMMER EDWARD

The Passing Over of Zephora

Trinidad & Tobago

Zephora awoke with a start. She rolled over and switched on the lamp. On the bedside table, next to the lamp, the skeleton watch lay face up, the moving parts mechanically counting down the ninth hour.

Three minutes past three.

She stared at the wardrobe that stood against the wall across from the foot of the bed, its doors locked. A huge oak wardrobe, like the one in the hall she remembered. Again, she wondered what was inside it, when last it had been opened, how long it had stood there, a piece of furniture as heavy and ominous as a coffin.

The window blinds were closed. Were it not for the watch, she would have no idea of the time. How long was it since she had left the plane? Groggy from the pills she had taken, she dug in her purse for the ticket. Good; a few hours remained until the next flight. She had a first-class ticket. She frowned; it was all wrong, she always flew coach . . .

All day, she had lain cold and stiff in the dim, air-conditioned room. While she had slumbered deeply, outside the island had grown golden with tropical afternoon light. Now, she warmed in the glow of the bedside lamp, (an unusual lamp, both base and shade golden, with a silver cord) and restlessness began to stir her blood. She showered and changed in the marble ensuite where the fragrance of Mediterranean countrysides, myrtle and aloe, drifted from a yahrzeit candle someone had left in the little alcove above the bath. Minutes later, after leaving the hotel lobby, she desperately longed for a glass of wine. A taxi was parked under the porte-cochère.

I've been waiting for you, the driver said in English, his Puerto Rican accent shaded with the formal quality of Canarian Spanish. He was dressed in black morning dress. Three initials gleamed from the monogram on his waistcoat: *J.R.J.* She stared at him for a moment, finding his appearance odd. There was no other taxi in the frontage of the hotel.

I only have an hour, she said. What do you recommend?

An hour? You must see Old San Juan then. You haven't been there? I'll take you . . .

Then they were breezing down Baldorioty de Castro Avenue, past the high-rise hotels of the Isla Verde. Then the taxi jounced along the cobblestoned streets of the Old World.

In Old San Juan, she sat at a table outside the Caficultura in a quiet, shaded corner of the Plaza de Colón. Through the tall, wood-framed windows of the old, Spanish-style building, windows with fanlights like doors, she could just make out the figures, but not the faces, of people dining in the dim interior.

A few empty *públicos* were parked on the south side of the square, their drivers idling in the shade. People crossed the plaza in groups or alone, scattering the pigeons as they went. She watched a man and woman pause by the fountain to take pictures of their children, twin boys wearing matching fisherman hats. An old woman dressed in mourning clothes sat on a bench, staring into space and fanning herself. These figures scattered about the plaza were just ordinary island people crossing a time-worn, familiar square, and yet to her they looked like players on a stage.

Her wrist felt naked without the skeleton watch; she had left it at the hotel. What was it about being here that made her feel uneasy about time? Perhaps it was the architecture. Tiled roofs, wrought-iron balconets, and *solistruncos* were familiar enough relics of the Spanish colonial past, yet these architectural relics seemed an irregularity in contemporary time. They made her presence in the old city seem like a form of *déjà vu*. These very thoughts, as she brooded beneath a patio umbrella in a Caribbean city, seemed like a glitch in the time-zone system. She could be in Córdoba, Granada, Seville. She could be timeless.

She craned her neck, looked upward at the red tile roofs. She had read somewhere that the tiles, the warm colour of a clay found in certain Mediterranean regions, were a Roman invention. Her eyes moved over the pastel-coloured walls of the buildings. Then it was she saw the man.

He stood on the balconet of the upper floor of the café across the street, hands resting on the ironwork balustrade. He was obviously a foreigner. He sported neither the traditional *guayabera*, nor the muscle shirt, bling, baggy jeans and *chancletas* of the healthy Puerto Rican male. His clothing was a nod to the American hippie of the sixties: Moroccan-style kaftan shirt, cotton gauze slacks, Birkenstock sandals. Except for the red *gorro* cap on his head, he was dressed coolly in white, even the Birkenstocks.

She noticed two things. First, that the man rested his hands on the balustrade with the palms facing upward. Was it a gesture of surrender or the relaxed posture of meditation? She noticed, too, that he had shut the balconet doors behind him. Why would someone come out onto a balconet and shut the doors? A mystery, like the shut doors of the hotel wardrobe. The man did not look at her.

A slight breeze ruffled the patio umbrella, then a large cloud drifted across the sun, deepening the shade. What time was it anyway? Some instinct caused her to reach into her pocketbook, and her fingers closed around the skeleton watch. So she had not left it at the hotel after all. Now she looked at the timepiece and found that the moving parts were frozen.

Time had stopped in the Plaza de Colón.

The sun came out again, brightening the world.

Excuse me, but would you believe me if I said you have saved my life?

The man was sitting across from her. He had been standing on the balconet only seconds ago it seemed, yet here he was. Now that he was closer, she could see he was older than she had thought. Old enough to be her father, almost an ancient air to his presence.

Look, she began. I am afraid I am not interested.

I saw you sitting here and I knew you were waiting for me.

Something about his speech stilled her. Somehow it was familiar to her. Like the taxi driver, he had a Puerto Rican accent but spoke easily in English.

How did you get down here so fast?

The man smiled. It did not seem to take forever then? My coming down to you?

No. I was not waiting for you. I did not even know you were watching me.

But *you* were watching *me*.

Zephora examined his face closely. There was a softness in his dark eyes that held her. It radiated to the high, flat brow and unsharpened the effect of the hollow almost deathly cheeks, assuring her of the man's beneficence. His straight, fair hair was cut short at the front and longer at the back, covering the ears. His face was clean shaven.

Well . . . I was wondering why you shut the doors behind you.

The doors?

Yes. The balcony doors. You came out onto the balcony and shut them behind you. It seemed a strange thing to do.

Yes, well I came out on that balcony to die, or rather, to kill myself. It was to be the final act. No, the curtain close, or is it curtain call? I don't know what it was that made me shut the doors. He spoke calmly, contemplatively. No, I do know. I wanted to shut out life, that is what. Yes, that is it. A symbolic gesture then. Let us say I wanted to shut out any possibilities that I would not go through with it. Shut out doubts and hesitations. Do you think that is true?

I don't know what is true for you. But you would not have fallen to your death. The balcony is not high enough.

A high death? A death not high enough? A high death, yes . . .

He seemed to be considering certain options, turning them over in his mind.

Is that what you wanted?

I only wanted to jump and get a little hurt. Scare myself a little perhaps?

I think so. Without knowing why, she felt deeply sorry for him. What is it? A woman?

Well . . . they will say it all started with the woman, yes. But no, it is much more. Much, much more. If you only knew.

Well, let us talk about something else. You look so sad. You are not from here?

I am from here in a way. Just like you are from here in a way.

In what way am I from here?

You are from a region where the nations share an overarching history. You belong more to a region than you do to a nation. You can travel anywhere along this chain of islands and find customs and traditions that remind you of your own. You recognize yourself in others, and everyone recognizes you.

She remembered the *déjà vu* that had disturbed her upon entering Old San Juan. Yes, I suppose you are right.

I, on the other hand—his gaze shifted outward, lingered on the taxi that was parked across the plaza, waiting to carry her back to the hotel in Carolina, in the New World—I am not very recognizable to most people here.

There was truth to his words. Looking at him, she could only guess at his background. The African-Caribbean paradox that wrestled in her own features did not make an appearance in his. He was not of a European cast. Was he Berber? Arabic perhaps? Those were the two races she associated with Moroccan people.

You are leaving soon.

She followed his gaze across the plaza. Her driver had gotten out of the car. He was leaning against the hood, smoking and staring passively in her direction.

Yes, I have to go soon. She realized she was still holding the skeleton watch. The gold-plated bezel had grown warm in her hand. Do you have the time?

You still have time, he said calmly. Do not worry. I would not keep you here if you did not have time.

She stared at him again, wondering why he seemed so familiar.

You were waiting for me, he said, returning to his earlier train of thought and here I am. I was waiting for you too. I see that now.

She did not know how to respond to this mysteriousness. She had realized she was connecting him with Morocco partly because of his kaftan shirt. Yet the kaftan could mean nothing at all. Funny, she thought, how the mind works. She could feel the delicate ratchets, bridges, and wheels of the timepiece pressed against her palm. Yes, the mind works mechanically, like clockwork or an engine. But the mind, like clockwork and engines, could fail without warning.

You are smiling. The foreigner's voice interrupted her thoughts. Now she realized it was his voice, not his manner of talking, that she recognized.

Your voice, she said. I seem to have heard it somewhere before. It rises and falls like the ocean waves . . .

That is nicely said. His eyes smiled at her from across the table. You speak very poetically. And I am a man of the seas, so that is fitting.

Oh, I *thought* you looked like a yachter! She laughed, pleased with herself. Is that what you are? Or are you a ship's captain?

I am a captain of souls, I am a master of fates . . . something like that . . . but you smiled just now. Why?

Was I? Oh, I was just thinking about assumptions, how funny they are. Your kaftan . . .

Yes, the kaftan meant *something*, she thought. Didn't everything? It was something she had first understood years ago, as a child, when she used to hide in the half-darkness beneath her sister's bed, or sit on the earth beneath her mother's oleander trees until she fell into a trance amidst the dragonflies that flew across the yard like little airplanes that never once collided.

I myself don't really have a style, she found herself saying.

I think you have style.

No, *a* style. I just mean . . . well. Her fingers fiddled with the watch. It's just that . . . I don't really know who I am.

I see. He fell silent then. He stared out at the sky and seemed to be carefully considering the matter. It is important to ask questions, he said finally. You are very good at that, yes?

She laughed again. I suppose I am.

And the answers do not always satisfy you?

I suppose they don't. Come to think of it . . . She sighed, suddenly feeling gloomy despite the brilliance of the tropical afternoon. I suppose they never do.

I will tell you this. Now, he leaned forward earnestly, as if he was about to take her into his confidence. Are you listening? It is most important to question everything. Be aware of your assumptions and question everything. Your life depends upon it, do you understand? You are young in a young world, and the young always assume; that is to be expected. But I tell you, the time is coming when your youth will seem like a dream. Perhaps you have begun to feel that way even now? That you are waking up from a dream? Yes, I can see it in your face! I want you to understand what I am saying. Do not worry too much about the answers. The answers are in the questions, you see? I saw you sitting below me, and I was about to perform my final act. You did nothing, just looked at me, and yet you saved my life. Do you see what I am saying? Look closely! The world is not what it seems. See these people? Since we have been talking, so many of them have left this stage. So it is, so it is. I am just saying, pay attention. That is all. Do not worry about the answers, they are illusions. It will make sense to you when you are my age. But I am telling you now, only to save you from so much misery. This is not easy to accept, I know. But you understand, don't you? Tell me, am I making sense to you?

I think . . . I think I do. But you are right. It is not easy.

Yes, well . . . He reached into a pocket for a silk handkerchief and wiped a few beads of sweat from his forehead. It is what is required of us.

She looked around the plaza. It was almost empty now. Out in the middle of the square, the Discoverer towered above the world on his marble pedestal, his sceptre raised to the sky, a cross finial poking through folds of marble banner.

Is it me or is it getting darker?

It is only a trick of the eye. He gazed into the café windows, and the look of sadness she had seen earlier returned. Like seeing through a dark glass . . .

She followed his gaze. Inside the cafe, made dim by the tinted pane, the faceless diners carried on their pantomime. She looked at him again. But you haven't told me much about yourself. Your name . . . ?

My name? What does it matter? I am who I am. As for the rest, I am a seaman without a home. I set sail from Andalucía many years ago . . .

Zephora awoke with a start. Something had jolted her out of her dream, and now there was a strange smell, the smell of something burning. Troubled, she glanced across the aisle, looking for the mother and child. Earlier, when she had entered the plane, she had smiled at the child and exchanged pleasantries with the young mother. But now they were gone. *What would become of them?* It felt like a sign, their disappearance. Always the symbols to taunt her, the archetypes, the omens. Her own mother was dead to her, in the metaphorical sense of the word.

Suddenly, she felt sick. Maybe it was the turbulence, or perhaps she was sick with understanding. She could only cradle herself and lean over in the seat. Emergency position. She recalled that there was nothing beneath her, only the far-fetchedness of air.

When, after a while, no one commented on her position, not even the first-class stewardess, an angel of a woman who hovered above her with a smile, Zephora gingerly raised her head. She took the glass of wine, although she had not asked for it. A strange sort of relief, this sense of not having made a choice. She took a few sips then gripped the armrest and stared out the porthole at the giant silver wings.

Her eyes felt heavy. The light inside the cabin began to take on a warm, vinaceous glow, and like so many times, when she had peered through the haze of dreams in the half-darkness beneath her sister's bed, the world around her began to seem unreal. The shutters on the airplane windows were sliding up and down, so they seemed to be blinking like eyes, and an unnatural light slowly filled the cabin, as if they were literally flying off into the sunset. Maybe I *am* a bit touched in the head, she thought ruefully. It was what her mother had said to the doctor when she was a child, and they had found her sitting on the ground beneath the oleander trees in the yard, eating the poisonous leaves.

She thought she heard a child screaming.

She remembered she was going to a new country, that things would be better there. To calm herself, she started humming the Disney song, the one about the magic carpet: *a whole new world.*

The blinding light grew brighter, brighter, then cooled to a most pleasant glow.

She is flying on the back of the giant dragonfly high above the valley, flying through the warmly glowing sky. With each lift of the creature's silver wings, there is a sweet fragrance, like the scent of oleander filling the air beneath her mother's trees.

They are heading for the grand mountains just ahead. From the central mountain, the tallest, a majestic waterfall hangs like a long white veil, stretching on and on into the wide river valley.

This is the loveliest place Zephora has ever been in all her flights and dreams. After what seems like centuries, but must really only be minutes, they reach a high, grassy plateau. There, the creature alights.

What is this place? Zephora asks, sliding to the ground.

If you go up the mountain, you will find all the answers. The creature's voice is like the sound of many waters. But if, however, you go down the mountain, then you will find the questions.

After the creature departs, Zephora hears its voice within her like the shadow of a repeating memory. Before her, the valley's flood plain is lush with grasses, its slopes exuberant with flowers, lily of the valley and red anemone. It stretches as far as eyes can see. Staring out at it, she cannot recall so vivid a green, brighter than the green light that would bleed from the leaves of her mother's trees when, as a child, she fell into a trance that made colours come alive.

Now, resting on the grassy highland above the river valley, puzzling over her choices (*Answers or questions. Go up the mountain or down.*), she falls into a reverie that gives her memories the ghostly patina of a seventeenth century phantasmagoria: visions of the dead and skeletons dancing through smoke. She remembers a yard fringed with oleander trees, the smell of dark earth, the earth of an island. She is a child, running from the yard to the house. Inside the house, crossing the dim, empty drawing room reserved for guests, lace doilies on the teapoys, antimacassars on the settees. Running past the wooden louvres that let in cool trade winds, her bare feet on the smooth rattan mat. The house is not architecturally significant, but the memory of the house has an architecture of its own, a strange, significant architecture, like missing walls and unstable rooms in dreams. *The symbols, the archetypes, the omens . . .*

But the memory is false. The drawing room is not empty. And she is not a child. She is eighteen years old, running away from the inquisition of her family. Her older sister Anara, the Real Beauty of the family, the remarkable and remarked upon, has won an island scholarship, has stolen the first boy she ever loved.

Are you thinking about the future, Zephora? Why don't you follow your sister's example? What will become of you? Stay in the island or go abroad. Take flight or don't take flight. Enter the plane or not. Sitting on the settee, across from her lovely, treacherous sister, the choices puzzled her. She is sitting calmly at the inquisition, then suddenly she is running away from it all, running through the unstable architecture of the collapsing house, running fast along the tarmac to the waiting plane.

The plane!

How long ago was it since she had entered the plane? It

could be moments or centuries. The choices puzzled her. What was more important, the questions or the answers?

Go up the mountain or down?

She placed the watch on the table. Already, she thought of the diners from the unreliable perspective of nostalgia. She saw them grow statuesque in her memory, black-and-white snap-shots rather than colourful, moving images. She closed her eyes and listened. Dusk was falling upon the old Caribbean city. From one of the trees in the square, a nightjar whistled mournfully. At the sound, she opened her eyes again, sighed heavily and tapped a finger to her wrist.

I still don't know the time, but I must go now.

I do not think you should get on that plane.

I have to.

You must not enter that plane, I feel sure of it.

The Andalucian was leaning back in his chair. His gaze was steady on hers and he spoke in a calm, unrushed way. She did not know whether to be amused or alarmed.

Why?

He thought for a moment. Let us say I have a feeling.

And what if I go anyway?

Earlier today, I walked down a hill to get here. Through the window of an upper floor room, I saw a woman in white clothes talking on the phone. She called to me and spoke to me from the window of the *entresol*. She told me I would meet you . . .

There was a long silence, during which he picked up the broken watch and examined it. Finally, he sighed. This place, the time, I know it is confusing. But is your choice. You have already made up your mind I see . . .

A few hours before, descending into the Luis Muñoz Marín International Airport, she had watched from above, the white caps of the Atlantic breaking against the shores of Carolina.

Carolina, named after the Bewitched king of Spain, la﹖
Habsburg rulers. Carolina, hometown of the great Latin
ican poet Julia de Burgos. Carolina, city of twenty-first cer
luxury resorts and American affluence, JC Penny and TJ M.
stores like rarefied rooms of heaven in the dazzling Plaza Ca.
olina. Puerto Rico, island of sixteenth century citadels, killer
rums, Cuban exiles. Borinquen, an island between two worlds.

A memory of a long-ago day on the island, a day when she had
visited an old abbey in the hills. She went alone, bearing her
loneliness. The buildings told her no secrets. She sat in the cool,
secretive mission, whitewashed walls and low ceiling, like hiding
out in a sea cave. Someone had left a missalette open on the pol-
ish-stained pew. Kneeling women all around, mute and solitary
in their supplication, grow statuesque in her memory.

Leaving, she walked down the winding mountain road in
the hot sun, the afternoon's palpable somnolence. From the
overhangs above the road, woman's-tongue trees dangled their
branches like the arms of sleeping people. She paused to look at
a small graveyard, the headstones so overrun by weeds she could
not read the names of the dead. She could hear children's voices,
faintly, in the distance. Walking on, she passed a preschool where
she could see in the upstairs window a woman in white clothes
talking on a rotary phone.

Further down the mountain, she paused to take pictures of
the view. There was no one to take her picture, so she stood the
camera on an ancient rock. She set the timer. She ran and sat below the green cliff-face, on the grass dappled with sunlight and
shadow. She laughed at nothing in particular. The countdown
seemed to take forever while she laughed and laughed, waiting
for the bright flash that never came.

A New Life in a New Time

Trinidad & Tobago

ernard Gray started each morning with a single boiled egg. It was served in a stainless steel eggcup with the words *Porrima Inc.* engraved around its centre band, and was often accompanied by a glass of lemon water which he would hurriedly gulp. He usually followed this with a small bowl of steel-cut oats.

Today, he was eager to reach this part of his breakfast, this new addition to his meal. In the centre of his grains sat half a maraschino cherry. Its colour had started to bleed out to the edges of the tiny Pyrex bowl. His gaze became transfixed on the thin pink strands blotting out the cream of his oats.

He swished the milky grains through his teeth, causing his tongue to be aroused by the moving textures. He looked at his clock and his throat tightened. He breathed slowly, closed his eyes and reminded himself that it was set twenty minutes fast and there was still plenty of time.

"Today I might see her," he said calmly to the bowl of oatmeal.

Suddenly his back was struck with pain, the sides of his abdomen were swollen. He passed his hand over his hanging stomach in an attempt to soothe the cramps as the food plummeted into it. He was dizzy. He took a deep breath.

The clock continued ticking while Bernard stared at it, the sound growing louder in the early morning silence.

Bernard gasped as oatmeal stuck to the back of throat. He choked and spat the loose grains back into his bowl. He moved towards the bathroom and the nausea began, his abdomen still cramping. He needed to urinate; and when he finally did, it came out like scraping blades and fire.

He took his clothes off, stepped into the shower and let the sweat wash off his body.

When Bernard got to work, he walked through the aisle between the cubicles of his co-workers and turned into his cubed space. He placed his bag with his lunch in a corner of his desk and took out his *Porrima Inc.* water bottle. He made a slow trek to the kitchen, counting his steps.

Thirty-five.

He winced and forced another step.

Thirty-six.

He began to fill his water bottle at the cooler. He consciously regulated his breaths, and reminded himself to go at it slowly. Slow. Smooth. And deep.

The heavy staccato tap of stilettos roughly stabbing the floor shook Bernard out of his calculated breathing.

His hands trembled severely enough to make the bottle spill water on the floor and on his shoes. He tried to steady his breathing. The taps stopped behind him and he heard the refrigerator open and close. He removed his bottle from the lever, cutting the flow of water, but remained with his back towards the refrigerator. With the sucking of teeth, the high heels wheeled on the floor with a harsh scrape and the taps faded from the kitchen.

Bernard held his breath. He closed the bottle and made his way back to his cube, counting his steps along the way.

Twenty-seven. The odd number bothered him.

He sank into his chair and sucked some water. He thought of all the things he would have to do that day. He would refill his bottle twice more, and urinate approximately seven times. Bernard's stomach groaned.

The computer's clock said 8:47 am.

He stared until it turned to 8:48 am before allowing his eyes to leave the screen.

On either side of him, Bernard could hear rapid typing and muffled conversations. He rolled his fingers over his pens aimlessly, and looked over to his lunch bag. Three more hours . . .

The tap of high heels scattered through the office hum, its pace different from before–angrily hurried.

Bernard's stomach began to cramp. The taps came closer and closer. His breathing became slow and deep. Slow. And deep.

His hand trembled over his mouse as he opened the spreadsheet he had completed the week before. *Porrima Inc. Promotional Item Inventory. 10,000 Porrima Inc. umbrellas ordered and received for this quarter. 30,000 pens, and 20,000 tote bags, all in assorted colours. Blue, black, red and yellow.*

The taps came to a jarring halt in front of Bernard's cubicle. He began to concentrate very hard on the spreadsheet in front of him, beads of sweat forming on his upper lip.

5,000 blue tote bags. 5,000 black tote bags, 5,000 red tote bags, and 5,000 yellow tote bags. 20,000 tote bags, in assorted colours.

He could hear her voice, not her words, but suddenly it rose to a shrill. He looked up at her pasty, wrinkled face.

"You're not listening to me, Bernard! I wonder if you remember your status here. I don't have to keep you here taking up my space!"

She hit the sidewall of his cubicle with her palm. Bernard winced. *Her* space.

He rolled his eyes to her badge, to see if her position had

changed. The flaking bronze-plated finish flashed dully: *Ms. Eris, Jr. Officer.*

He stared at her as she spoke. The yellow plaque accumulated at the base of her teeth glistened under the fluorescent lighting. He rested his eyes on her mouth, watching her tongue roll in a pond of her saliva as her voice melted into the background. She concluded suddenly with a stamp and a scream.

He watched her leave and then left for the bathroom. His vomit painted the bowl beige with tinges of pink.

Bernard spent the rest of his morning drinking water and urinating while reviewing spreadsheets with hundreds of tiny petty numbers always adding up to the final significant number.

At midday, he got up from his seat, taking his lunch bag with him. He took the elevator to the twelfth floor and knocked on the door labelled *Tech Support.* He adjusted his tie and smoothed his yellow and brown plaid trousers. The door unlocked with a loud beep and swung open. Derrick was on the other side with his arms folded, giving Bernard a quizzical look through his thick lenses.

"What did she blame you for this time?" Derrick asked. He stepped aside to let Bernard in.

"I don't know," Bernard said, pulling a chair out. "I stopped listening," He rustled his whole wheat and egg sandwich out of his bag. "She hit the cubicle wall again. I . . . I think I dislike her."

Derrick crumpled his face as the scent of the egg reached his nostrils. "You can hate her, I don't care."

Bernard placed a serviette over his trousers and took a huge bite out of the sandwich.

Derrick crinkled his nose at Bernard before continuing. "She's an asshole. She's been here for a long time holding a shit position, but she yells at all the young officers to feel important." He flicked open a can of soft drink. "She thinks shouting at you is her reward for her thirty years of service." He took a huge gulp.

"People who have little power are eager to exert it on others," Bernard said, staring at the floor and taking another bite. "So . . . are you going down there today?"

"Down where?" Derrick asked. He had put the soft drink down and was now typing rapidly on his keyboard.

"You know where," Bernard said softly as he turned his face away from Derrick. "Basement 8."

Derrick grinned. "Aching to see her, aren't you? Chamber Eighty-Eight."

Bernard shifted in his seat. "Her name is Ava." But Eighty-Eight wasn't such a bad number to describe her as. It made him feel light.

Derrick got up and ruffled Bernard's thick curls. "You're one lucky bastard. Paul's out sick so I'm going down today."

Bernard's face lit up.

"C'mon." Derrick pulled a black key card out of pocket. "Let's go talk to the dead."

Bernard crumpled his sandwich into his bag as he followed Derrick out the door and into the elevator. Derrick swiped the key card in front of the scanner and they began to descend into the underground floors, stopping at Basement 8.

As Bernard stepped out he shivered, a dull blue light falling across his face. His lips slowly parted as his eyes adjusted to the darkness. A night sky was painted on the walls of the large room. Stars and moons covered in wisps of cloud. Directly in front of him were several thick cables, connected to an enormous metal cube, and as he walked towards them he could hear the whirring of machinery. His breath came out like white smoke from his lips. Bernard felt something heavy fall over his shoulders. Derrick had put a parka over him.

Derrick's glasses looked dark against the blue light, and with the huge jacket over him, Bernard thought he looked like an Arctic explorer.

"C'mon, the computer is in the back there. And remember, don't touch anything, Bernard. They only check the cameras if they detect something's wrong."

Bernard nodded and put his arms through the huge jacket's sleeves.

They walked around to the other side of the giant cube, huge sheets of glass lying over it. It looked like a massive refrigerator. Bernard recalled his orientation course—he remembered being guided through the client entrance. Derrick had led them through the maintenance entrance.

Derrick pulled up a chair behind the main computer and swiped his card to turn it on. Combinations of symbols flashed up on the screen and Derrick began swiftly typing lines of code.

Bernard stepped quietly away from him while he did this. The first time he had come down to the Cryonics Floor of Porrima Inc. was during his orientation course where the new communications and marketing officers were introduced to the product they would be selling: *A New Life in a New Time.*

After extensive research confirmed that revival from cryopreservation was not only plausible, but more widely accessible, both in the means of biological revitalisation and the successful integration of the Awakened into present society, Porrima Inc. began an aggressive marketing campaign to encourage a new kind of clientele.

Cryonics was no longer for the extravagant, the rich, and the eccentric, who wanted to live in the very distant future, but for the common man who found that his life was currently in a slump. The daydream of a *time skip* just a couple years into the future was now reality; it provided an escape from the current situation.

It was around that time that Porrima Inc. made a grand call to all qualified persons to join their company, and boost their communications and marketing department. Bernard had seized this opportunity more than a year ago.

He barely remembered the tour around the building until they were scanned and sterilised before entering the Cryonics Floor. Their CEO, Dr. Carmenta, was a man who thought strategically. He understood that one of the most important things within a company was the dissemination of information from top to bottom; every member of the company's staff should have a basic knowledge of how the company worked and what their goals and visions were. However, for Marketing and Sales, Dr. Carmenta thought that it was most important that they got the full tour, the meat of the meal, their frozen cash cow.

Bernard thought he was going to faint the first time he came down to the Cryonic Floor. He could see the faces of all their clients through the glass windows of their separated chambers. They were grey with their eyes wide open and their blue lips slightly ajar. Their wrinkled faces sagged over their old bones.

These were the frightened magnates who were looking for one last avenue to escape the unknown of death. They were the *long-termers* or the *Dead-Sleepers*. They were put away, waiting for the future that could hopefully cure them. Make them young again so that they could relive the decadence of youth. Bernard understood that he would be an old man when the time came for their revival. But these were not the ones he was looking for.

He was looking for the *short-termers*, the ones who were put away for just a couple years to escape the pain of the present, to be awakened when those agonies had passed. Bernard left Derrick behind the main computer and headed to the smaller chambers for the *short-termers*.

The sound of Derrick's typing faded.

"Don't touch anything, man," Derrick's warning echoed in the darkness.

Bernard kept on walking, counting his steps, checking the smaller chamber boxes for the increasing numbers. He couldn't believe people did this, that they hid themselves away for a couple years because they hated the current state of their lives. Because they hated themselves? No matter how bad things got, he could never do this. He could never hide himself away from the world, especially when he had something to look forward to every day.

Bernard stopped.

She was wrapped in the fetal position like all the short-termers. Her formerly shaven head had sprouts of black, tightly-curled hair covering her scalp. Bernard looked through the glass for the tattoo on her left shoulder. He could only see the top, her head and a bit of her arm.

He leaned against her chamber, the coldness of the glass penetrating through the back of his parka, and rested his head back.

"Ava, it's Bernard. I'm having a bad day."

Bernard woke up with Derrick's shoe nudging him against his calf. "Hey man, it's time to head back up."

Bernard nodded and slowly picked himself off the ground. He looked at Ava's face one last time before accompanying Derrick to the twelfth floor.

Returning to his own desk, he saw his phone lighting up. He slipped on his headset. "Good day, Porrima Incorporated, we offer you a new life in a new time! Bernard speaking."

". . . I don't know if this is a good idea." The woman at the other end was sobbing.

"This is the best idea you've had today . . ." Bernard glanced at the phone screen. "Yvonne, it's a great idea. Today, things didn't go so great, am I right?" Bernard clicked his browser and began skimming through his emails.

"How did you . . ." Her breathing had already accelerated into hyperventilating gasps. "It's more like nothing went well this whole month, this whole year. I hate everything right now. I want to make it stop, I want everything to stop. I want everyone to stop looking at me make every single mistake I can. I hate my life!"

"Everything is better tomorrow, Yvonne, and we can help you reach there faster." Bernard's stomach cramped as he registered the red exclamation mark on the email.

"It's gotta be better than this shit."

"I promise it will be, Yvonne. Let me transfer you to our bookings department. You're about to have a wonderful future to wake up to."

Bernard tapped in some keys and hung up the phone. The words were red and large on the screen. *See Me*. He left his cubicle and entered the elevator. He came out at the twenty-seventh floor. The number bothered him. He signed his name at the secretary's desk and headed towards the office at the end of the long corridor. He walked slowly, measuring his steps in sets of twenty. At the first step he took a long breath, at the tenth step he exhaled very slowly, there was a pause at twenty as if he was deciding whether to breathe again.

The wooden door felt warm and smooth on his knuckles as he knocked. The door clicked and he entered. Ms. Eris was seated on the couch behind an oval coffee table laden with biscuits and iced wedges of cake. She was absentmindedly picking at her teeth, but immediately straightened up as her eyes flickered over Bernard.

He cleared his throat and deliberately stood with his legs slightly apart. He did not know what to do with his arms. He touched his chin and then felt for his pen in his front pocket and realised he hadn't brought any sort of writing pad to this meeting.

Dr. Carmenta emerged from behind his enormous executive chair. He straightened up to his full height and pushed his long black hair over his shoulder, revealing a 12mm ear plug stretcher. He had a gentle smile on his face, speaking with a soft yet deep voice, "Glad you could come up here to see me." It was a languid purr, floating through the room.

"Yes, sir," Bernard said, his arms suddenly finding themselves at his side, his head erect. "It's a pleasure to meet with you, sir."

Dr Carmenta curled the ends of his hair around his left index finger.

"I'm sure you know Alexa," he said, gesturing towards Ms. Eris. "She has been giving me some interesting stories about your work . . . relationship. Alexa has been with us since my mother was our chief executive here and I would like her to be treated with respect."

There was a smack behind him as a lipstick-smeared mouth sucked inward into a smirk. Bernard kept his gaze ahead. There was a huge window behind Dr. Carmenta's chair, where the city stretched out like a map before him. Everything below moved slowly.

"Bernard, please, sit with us. Let's talk about this." Dr. Carmenta gestured towards the empty seat next to Ms. Eris. Dr. Carmenta sat in an armchair while Bernard miserably sank into the couch.

"Please, Bernard," Dr. Carmenta said, pointing to the slices of cake, "help yourself."

"I'm fine for now, sir."

"Bernard, let's make this a bit more casual. Have a slice of cake." Dr. Carmenta leaned forward and pushed a plate of enormous chocolate cake wedges towards Bernard.

Bernard exhaled slowly, took up a napkin and manoeuvred a slice into the pair of tongs. He brought the napkin-swaddled cake to his lips and bit off the edge. He stared into the wall shelves, chewing slowly as Dr. Carmenta began his introduction. There were two leather-bound copies of *Sleeping Beauty* next to a photo of Dr. Carmenta and his mother, Dr. Julia Carmenta.

Words crawled over the walls and the ceiling above Bernard:

Mediation, Work Together, Impossible, Tolerance, Respect.

The final word lingered in his ears as he swallowed the paste on his tongue.

The sugar burned the walls of his stomach. He released a tiny gasp as he registered the familiar pain and placed the cake back on the table.

"I would like to say something about this," Ms. Eris said as she struck her hand against her chest. "Since the first day that Bernard came here, I've been good to him. But in return he has embarrassed me countless times, correcting me in front of supervisors . . ."

Bernard heard her recount an incident that had happened a year ago, and slowly allowed her voice to disappear into the background as he contemplated the books on the shelf. Sleeping Beauty, a woman in a deep sleep awakened with a kiss, perhaps that was what everyone in those frozen coffins was waiting for.

"I tell him good morning and he doesn't even look at me!" Ms. Eris shrieked.

Dr. Carmenta shifted in his seat and tilted his head. Bernard's eyes moved between them.

"What do you have to say about this?" Dr. Carmenta said, smiling at Bernard.

"I apologise. I seem to have aggravated Ms. Eris. I've never meant to do these things. I will try harder to communicate in a more sincere fashion."

"Bernard, these things have been going on for months, and it seems that Alexa is beyond aggravated. She is grieved. She is developing . . . medical repercussions from your behaviour."

Bernard stared at Dr. Carmenta. His stomach suddenly clenched in a spasm.

"I'm going to try my best, sir."

"Bernard, are you familiar with our mediation clause in your contract?" Dr. Carmenta dug his chin into his open palm as Bernard shook his head. "It states that in circumstances where there are uncomfortable relations between colleagues, we work on them the one way we can. Time apart."

". . . Am I being suspended?"

"Bernard, we're creating a booking for you for twenty-two months in Basement 6. These are the terms that Ms. Eris has put forward to regain her emotional and physical wellbeing."

Bernard began to crumple. "You can't . . . do this. Can't you just suspend me?"

"This is for your own sake. It's rehabilitation for your behaviour. It's best we do it now before it gets worse."

"But you can't do this . . ."

"Yeah, they can." Derrick leant back in his chair and emptied his soft drink down his throat. "It's under their mediation thing where it's seen as rehabilitation, and it's preferred over firing or having an employee quit with their problems unresolved."

"But that's not true! We both know that you wake up with everything exactly the same! Nothing will change, Derrick!" Bernard began to gasp and buried his face in his hands. He was crying now.

Derrick shifted in his seat. "There was a girl who worked here a while back. She actually punched a manager who trapped her in the fireproof room to . . . you know. They gave her four years. But like you said, she's going to come out of that chamber with all that rage afresh. This isn't to help you, Bernard. This is for them to rid themselves of the guilt of their own behaviour. They hide you away and turn you into an icicle in the basement."

"I don't . . . I don't . . ." Bernard couldn't breathe. Derrick pushed a bottle of water into his hands and watched Bernard gulp it down.

"I don't want to be in that cold coffin. My life isn't like that, it's not like *theirs* . . ."

Derrick wheeled his chair slightly closer to Bernard. "Do you know . . . the chamber number?" he asked quietly.

Bernard raised his head up from his hands, "Sixty-eight, Basement 6." His assigned numbers made it all the more real. "Sometimes, I think that my life is terrible, that I don't want to do this anymore. But I realise I just lead a simple life and I do enjoy simple things. It's only when I compare myself to other people that I get depressed. It's now that I'm faced with this threat of having almost two years of my life blacked out that I realise how much I have and want to do right now."

Derrick nodded and opened up another can of soft drink.

Bernard continued, "I wanted to see Ava. One day, I wanted to see her awake and unfrozen. I wanted to hear her voice. What if she wakes up, leaves the building and I never get to hear her voice?"

Derrick extended his arm and patted Bernard on the back. "I wouldn't worry about that too much."

"It doesn't matter, does it? She wouldn't know who I was if she saw me. "

"Well, how about you get to hear my voice while you're in there. I'll let you know how things are doing."

Bernard took a long look at Derrick. "I would be happy if you did that for me."

Derrick stood before the main computer in the cold darkness, striking keys and reading lines of code. His breath came out as white clouds and floated out towards the chambers.

"What number is your friend's number again?" a voice echoed out between the chambers.

"It's sixty-eight," Derrick called back.

Ava walked through the chambers, looking at the numbers until she came to the window of a young man with a thin face. His cheeks were gaunt and his lips were slightly parted. He wore a pained expression with furrowed brows and squeezed eyes. Perhaps it was fear.

"You haven't got it so bad. I've been gone for four years. It's over in a second. Well, it feels like a second. You won't even real-ise that the world is changing around you because nothing inside you will change."

She touched the window of his chamber and made a dot in the condensation, when suddenly the observatory window di-rectly above glowed white. There was a tour happening for po-tential short termers. Ava shrank into the shadows, peeking out at the group.

The tour members stood near the glass, scanning the rows and rows of chambers. A woman walked towards the glass and pressed her hands against it. Her lips curled in a soft smile of hope, but her large brown eyes read only of desperation.

fallenangel.dll

Trinidad & Tobago

"Didn't have any problems getting back?"

Imtiaz stretched on the couch and sighed. "Nah," he called back to the kitchen. "Traffic was remarkably light today. You know how it is—takes a while for everyone to find their rhythm."

"I don't know how it is, actually," Tevin shouted from the kitchen. There was a rustle of plastic bags, and then he poked his head from the door. "I never experienced a state of emergency before."

"A blessing for which you should thank God," Imtiaz said. "I would've killed for the chance to study abroad when the last one happened. Worst three months of our lives."

After even more shuffling from the kitchen, Tevin came into the living room, a cold bottle of beer in each hand, and kissed Imtiaz on the cheek. "And was there a good reason for the last one?"

"Just as good a reason as this one."

Tevin sighed and handed his partner a bottle. "I guess I should have gotten more beer then."

Imtiaz chuckled. "Slow down, hoss. Since when you turn big drinker, anyway?"

"Country gone to the dogs? No better time, I figure." Tevin raised his bottle before him as a toast.

"To the dogs. Now they get to see us trapped at home." He brought his bottle to Tevin's with a soft clink, and then put it to his lips and took a long swig. It had only been three days so far since the Prime Minister had declared the country under lockdown, and everyone knew what a joke looked like when they saw it. It had been seven years at least since the last time he'd been in one, and the excuse was the same. "We are working hard with the Armed Forces," the Prime Minister would say, "to curtail the growing crime rate in this country, and we ask only that the citizens of this great twin-island state be patient in this effort."

The first thing that popped up on social media was also the most accurate: "How you does curtail crime by simply asking criminals to stay inside?"

Imtiaz felt a vibrating in his pocket, and reached into it for his cell phone. Almost as soon as he saw the text on his screen, he shoved it back into his pocket.

"Everything okay?" Tevin asked.

"Yeah." A long sigh, then Imtiaz took another, longer gulp of beer.

"Im?"

". . . It's nothing."

"If I have to ask what nothing is—"

Imtiaz frowned and put his drink down. "I just might have to head out in a bit."

Tevin squinted. Imtiaz didn't like getting in fights, least of all with Tevin, whose disappointed glares had the power to make him feel ashamed for days afterward. "I don't want to, but I kinda promised—"

"Promised who?"

"A friend of mine wanted help moving something. She doesn't want to talk about it." He got up and walked slowly to his bedroom. "I wish I didn't have to, but I promised before this was a thing–"

"But you can say no? It's minutes past six. You can't just head back out–"

"I promised," Imtiaz called back. "And I swear, it's not a big deal. Lemme just take care of it, and I'll be back before you miss me." He took the phone back out and opened the text this time: *so im at uwi, can you meet me at the gate?*

"Im." When he turned to the door, Tevin was already in the walkway, arms folded. "Come nah man. You wanna break curfew and not even tell me why?"

Imtiaz reached for a shirt hanging on the door of his wardrobe and put it over his grey tee. "It's Shelly. She said she needed someone with a car to help her move something two weeks ago, and now is the only day it can happen. I volunteered."

"'Move something'? What?"

"One of her projects. I dunno what yet."

There it was–Tevin's dreaded glare, as he tapped his foot on the white tile of the walkway. "A'right. A project. But if the police hold you, you're out of luck. And don't play like you taking your time to answer the phone if I call. You hear?"

"Yes, boss," Imtiaz said, a small smirk on his face. It was his only line of defence against Tevin's sternness. It didn't succeed often, but when it did, it did so well.

Tevin tried to fight the grin spreading over his face, and lost. "Be safe, Im. Please. Promise me that. Since you insist on keeping promises."

Imtiaz walked up to him, still slipping the last buttons into their holes, and kissed his partner softly on the lips. "I absolutely positively promise. I'll be fine."

"You bet your ass you'll be fine," Tevin whispered. "Play you're not going and be fine, see what I go do to you."

* * *

Imtiaz sped down the highway at sixty, seventy miles an hour, past the three or four motorists still making their way back home who glanced at him with fear. A dusty navy-blue Nissan rushing past in the dark night blaring circa-2007 noise rock does that to people.

He made sure to call before he took off. He'd meet Shelly at the South Gate and take off immediately. She asked if the back seat was empty, and if his boyfriend knew what they were going to pick up. Imtiaz reminded her that he didn't know either, to which she replied, "Oho, right—well, see you just-now," and hung up. This wasn't a good sign, but the volatile mix of curiosity and dedication to keeping his promises got the better of him.

It was twenty to seven when he pulled up, screeching to a halt right in front of the short Indian girl in the brown cargo pants and black t-shirt. She took the lollipop out of her mouth and peeped through the open driver-side window, putting a finger of her free hand into her ear to block out the music.

"You just always wanted to do that, right?"

"Get the *hell* in," he sneered.

"Alright, alright," Shelly said. She lifted a black duffel bag off the ground beside her and got in the back.

"Wait." Imtiaz turned back to face her. "What's in the bag?"

"Tools." She patted it gently as she said it, looking right at him, sporting a smug grin.

"Tools? Open it, lemme see."

"What, you think I selling drugs or somet'ing?"

"I t'ink if you weren't selling drugs, you'd be able to open the blasted bag."

Shelly slapped the bag even harder, just so he could hear the clanging of metal within. Her hand recoiled painfully. "Happy now?"

"No." He faced front and slowly got back on the road. "Where are we heading?"

"Eh . . . Just keep going west, I'll let you know."

"That isn't how you ask people to give you a lift."

Shelly sighed, rolling the lollipop from one side of her mouth to the next. "Would you get nervous if I said Laventi—"

"Laventille?" he shouted. "You want to go to *Laventille* at minutes to seven on the third night of a curfew? What, not being arrested or murdered is boring?"

"Trust me, when you see it, you'll be glad you came." Shelly grinned even wider. "Something you couldn't imagine. I could've gone myself, but didn't you wonder why I asked if you could do it? Not because I needed a car." She shrugged. "Although we will."

"Are you gonna tell me what it is?"

"Shh. You go see it." She shifted the duffel bag and lay across the length of the seat. "I dare you tell me you not impressed when we reach there." She winced, turning to face the stereo deck. "How you could listen to *this*?"

Imtiaz couldn't help but smirk. They'd spent many an afternoon debating the musical value of his thrashing, clanging metal music. At her most annoying, he wasn't beyond blasting it just to get on her nerves. Today felt as good a time as any.

"It calms me," he replied. It did. He imagined his thoughts dancing to it, his large sweaty moshpit of anxieties.

"I don't see how this could calm anyone, Im. It sounds like two backhoes gettin' in a fight."

"If you say so." He would have liked to describe the meaning of the present song at length—about rebellion, about sticking it to the man and rising above oppression and propaganda to finally live in a land where you were a free and equal citizen—but he had been Shelly's friend long enough to know that she didn't care. She appreciated that she had friends like Imtiaz who thought as deeply about the things they loved as she did about her own loves, but she never really wanted to know what those deep thoughts were. That would involve caring about the things they loved as well. She often didn't. Passionate people were more interesting to her than their passions.

He glanced at his watch, and panic shot through him. "Shit!" He swerved, aiming for an exit into a side street in San Juan.

"What the—?" Shelly bumped her head on the door, then straightened up.

"Why did I do this?" Imtiaz's eyes opened wide. "We going to get arrested!"

"Whoa!" Shelly put up her hands. "Don't panic. We came off the bus route, no one going to see us now. I go give you directions, okay?"

He lowered the volume on the stereo. "I don't like any of this, Michelle."

She winced at the sound of her whole first name. "I know. I should've say something before. But would you have come if I didn't?"

"What could be so important?"

"You really have to see it."

She pointed out the route, giving vague directions as if she were guessing at them, only appearing to get a better sense of where they were going as they got closer to the house. Shelly said she often passed through this area to look for the person they were meeting. She had met the man on a forum early last year. He was one of the few seemingly deluded souls to believe the government rumours of drones and police riot-suppression bots. This interested her less for anarchist, anti-establishment reasons, and more because this was her only chance to get to see a bot up close—if the rumours were true. Almost every month her friend would have some evidence, and almost every week he'd need to be bailed out of Golden Grove Prison for a heroin possession that wouldn't stick. Imtiaz asked if she trusted her friend, and she shook her head.

"That is why *we* going." Shelly was still focusing on the road when she said it.

Imtiaz focused on the road, too. Along the way, he had noticed at least three police jeeps. It looked like they were circling the area. He swore, too, that he'd heard a helicopter above, after leaving the San Juan border, but he couldn't hear it any more.

"We almost there," Shelly said, pointing at a rusted shack of galvanised sheeting, with a glittering lime-green sedan parked outside. "By that car." Imtiaz nodded, parked behind it, unplugged his phone, and got out. Shelly shuffled a bit inside before taking up her bag and opening the door. "Follow me. Lemme do the talking."

Imtiaz closed the door behind her and gestured for her to lead the way, past the car, past the front door to the side entrance. Shelly knocked three times, and a stern woman's voice shouted, "Just come inside, nah!"

The door swung open with a creak and Shelly stepped in, Imtiaz following close behind. He was hypervigilant, even to the point of being aware of his awareness, of whether he'd come across as nervous even as he glanced around for the faintest sign of threat. They were in the kitchen, which was better furnished than the outside of the house suggested—stainless steel sink, tiled countertop, the best dishwasher money could buy, even two double-door fridges.

A tall, dark woman was at the counter, dicing a tomato with a chef's knife. She looked fit, with beautiful soft features, with skin that wrinkled almost imperceptibly at the corners of her lips and near her eyes. Imtiaz guessed she was around her late fifties.

"Ey, it's Shelly!" the woman said, smiling but not taking her eyes off the tomato. "And who's your friend?"

"Missus Atwell, this is Imtiaz. You know how your son and I like putting together puzzles. Imtiaz likes that sort of thing, so I invited him to help."

"Ah, yes . . ." Ms. Atwell put down the knife and stared wistfully off into the TV room, where some soap opera was playing on mute. "Runako and his blasted puzzles. He does still never let me see them, you know. Even when the police take him, he insist—nobody mus' go back in his room an' look for anyt'ing."

"Yeah, the puzzles are kinda important, miss."

Ms. Atwell continued gazing distantly for a beat or two, and then went back to her tomato. "Well, just try not to stay too late. You getting a ride out of here after?"

"Yes, miss," Shelly said, nodding as she left the kitchen, gesturing for Imtiaz to follow down the short hallway to a dark brown door. Shelly rapped on it three times. They could hear the sound of large containers being dragged across the floor, and then one, two, three bolt locks being opened.

The door opened a crack, and a dark-skinned face poked through. His eyes were wide at first, but then he glanced at Shelly and sighed calmly, pulling the door open slowly. "Oh, it's you. Thanks for passing through."

"Of course I must pass through," she said as she entered, Imtiaz behind her. "You say you had something for me to see. I saw the picture. I just want to make sure."

Runako was a tall black man, perfectly baldheaded, in a white Jointpop t-shirt and black sweatpants. When he noticed Imtiaz looking at him, he nudged Shelly and stepped back, leaning on the wall nervously. "Who is this? Your friend?"

"Yeah. Runako, meet Imtiaz. He's the one going to help me put this back together. If you didn't set me up like all the other times."

He folded his arms. "Okay. But I telling you, too many times I get hold, I get lock up, because somebody tell somebody and the police hear. This is probably my last chance for somebody to see it."

Imtiaz had focused on an odd shape in the corner of the

room under a sheet of grey vinyl. When he turned back to the other two, they were glancing at it too. "This is it?" he asked.

Runako nodded. "Look at it, nah, Shelly? Exactly as I promised."

She stepped toward it and pulled the dusty vinyl off. In a coughing fit, her eyes widened as she looked at it. When she got her breath back, she turned to Runako. "Really?"

"See?!" Runako grinned. "I is not no liar."

"Imtiaz, come!" She waved to her friend to come closer, and he stepped up beside her. It was a robot with a matte black shell and glossy black joints. It had suffered severe damage; frayed wires poked out of an arm, its chestplate had a fist-sized hole in it. Imtiaz noticed that on its back were a pair of camouflage-green retractable wings; they looked as if they would span half the room when opened, maybe even wider. On its neck was a serial number painted in white stencil: TTPS-8103-X79I.

"TTPS?" Imtiaz said, almost at a whisper. "As in—"

"Yeah, man," Runako said behind them.

"A real live police bot . . ." Shelly straightened up slowly, dusting herself off. "This is the riot team model?"

"Yeah. The mark-two, in fact. Tear gas and pepper spray nozzles in the arm, but they not full, and stun gun charges; thrusters under the wings so it could dispense over crowds by flying overhead. Recording cam in one of the eyes—can't remember which, supposed to be forty megapixels. And some other things, but I didn't open it up yet. I was waiting for you."

Shelly rubbed her hands and reached down beside her to open the duffel bag and take out a long, flat-head screwdriver. "Why, thank you, kind sir. Now, gimme my music there. Time to start."

Runako nodded and stepped over to a stereo at the corner of the room. Shelly took a USB drive out of her back pocket and tossed it at him. He caught it, slotted it in a back port, and pressed a couple of buttons. He stepped back as something haunting and atmospheric played, the lyrics lo-fi and echoing, the instrumental thumping and dark. Shelly swayed a little as the sound rumbled through the room, eyes closed, facing the ceiling, as if taken briefly by some heavenly rapture. Then she straightened and pointed her screwdriver at Imtiaz. "You hear that, Immy? Now that is music to calm you. Not whatever wildness you does listen to."

Imtiaz squinted, eager to ask what made her witchy-sounding, incomprehensible music better than his tastes, but he kept his question to himself.

Shelly knelt before the thing and started unscrewing the outer panels, observing the wiring as it snaked across its chest and limbs, leading to each gear or tool it powered. Imtiaz pulled up a chair by the wall so he could see, but not so close as to disturb her.

Her hands moved as if she were in a trance. Gently, screws would slowly wind out of their places, plating would fall into her hands, she would gently place it beside her on a sheet of newspaper on the floor. She would follow the lines of red and green and purple wire from the processor in its headpiece to the battery supply in its centre and then out to the extremities, to its tear gas canister launchers, its sensory databases. Imtiaz thought that they looked like the veins of . . . . Of course they did. Of course they looked like veins, like nerves, like sinews. What else could a man do but copy?

He stared at the serial number on a sheet of plate on the floor. A police riot bot. Here, in Laventille. On a night of curfew. He went from peacefully admiring Shelly's diligence right back into panic.

Shelly said softly, "You're gonna be checking the BIOS after this is done, by the way. So get a laptop ready. Runako?"

Runako snapped a finger, then picked up a dusty grey notebook near the stereo. "Here, boss." He took a couple of long steps to get to Imtiaz and rested it in his lap.

As Imtiaz opened it, he could hear Shelly mumbling to herself about "not that much damage", and the bot being "up and running in an hour". He glanced up to see that most of the outer shell, save for the wings, were gone, the bot's innards entirely visible. He could see past them to the bedroom wall. It was almost a work of art as it was.

He opened a guest profile on the laptop and launched a web browser. "How you paying for this, again?" he said.

"'You'?" Shelly chuckled. "You mean *we*."

"What?" He froze for a moment. "No. No, I don't. Trus' me, I don't."

"So . . . I forgot to mention . . ." She had a pair of pliers in hand now, stripping some of the power-supply wires with them.

"Mention *what?*"

"I promised Runako we would come back if he needed anything. In exchange for this."

"Wha–" He wanted to shout, but he glanced at Runako and decided against it. He didn't know what kind of person he was dealing with. As the host folded his arms, Imtiaz cleared his throat. "You didn't think this was probably worth sharing with me first? Before even asking me to come here?"

"I figured it wasn't going and be a problem. You like them kinda thing."

"But I don't like doing it *for free* for people I *don't know*."

Shelly gestured to the robot with a free hand. "Look–it already open. We already here. I asking nicely. This is too big an opportunity."

He didn't answer right away, but he wanted to say no. This was the neighbourhood where strangers got shot. He wasn't planning to come back, national lockdown or not "How much something like this supposed to cost?"

Shelly had already returned her focus on the wiring. "This is seven figures at least."

Runako chimed in. "Black market is nine hundred fifty thousand."

Imtiaz sighed as softly as he could, too softly for them to hear. He couldn't do it. His skin felt tight against him, his palms clammy and warm. He logged into Facebook in the hope of finding something silly and distracting while Shelly tended to the robot.

The very first shared link on his feed read *Sources Warn of Police Raids in Hotspots to Curb Crime During Curfew*. He opened it in another tab: "Residents in several so-called 'crime hotspots' across the island have claimed that their areas are being targeted by police officers who, as part of their crackdown on crime, are performing random house searches for illegal contraband . . ."

Imtiaz felt his chest get tight. He glanced at the window and was sure he could see flashing blue lights several streets away. He glanced back at the article: "Several Western areas, such as Belmont and Laventille, are due for their own random searches at the time of posting, sources say." He heard a siren blare suddenly, and just as suddenly, silence. He was sure.

"You nervous or what, man?" Runako said sternly.

"What?" Imtiaz turned to face him. "Nah, I good."

"You sure? Like you freaking out about the deal."

He looked away, hoping to hide whatever signs of fear were on his face. "I just could've been told before, that's all."

"Ey." Runako snapped his fingers, and Imtiaz twitched. "What? You is another one of them who feel they too good for Laventille?"

"I didn't say that." Imtiaz got out of his seat and walked to the bedroom window, pulling the curtains open only enough to get a good view. The street was empty and dimly lit. "Although you can't blame a guy, can you?"

"What that supposed to mean?"

"It supposed to mean people don't like coming to places and being afraid they not going and make it back home after."

"Really?" Runako folded his arms. "This is the fool you go look to bring in my house, Shelly? During de curfew, no less, a man going and tell me the whole of Laventille not safe for nobody?"

"You hear me say—"

Shelly whistled, still not looking up from the robot. "Fellas, I like a good rousing sociopolitical debate just like everybody else, but we on a clock, right? So cool it."

Runako backed off, but Imtiaz kept looking out of the window. This time he was positive—a police jeep stopping at the top of the street, one man coming out of the back seat and shouting at the window of a house. "I don't like this."

Shelly was already taping over some exposed wires, and taping around them all to keep them in place. "I'm almost done, Im. You'll just check the firmware quick, help me load it into the car, and that's it. We almost finished."

Imtiaz saw the officer beat on the door of the house until a woman came out, and then grab her by the neck and throw her out onto the street. He shouted again. Another officer came out from the driver's side door, a pistol already in his hand.

"Stop almost-finishing and *finish*, then," he said nervously. "Trouble up the street."

She looked over the inside of the shell again, tracing her hands along all the snaking wires, trying to find a spot she had overlooked. When she couldn't find one, she shrugged, beginning to screw each plate of its iron skin back together. "We could deal with the outer damage when we take it home, I guess. Your turn."

It took Imtiaz a moment to peel away from the window. The second officer had just struck a small child in the head with his handgun, and his partner was already barging into the house. Imtiaz sighed and got back to his chair. "You have a Type C cable?"

For a moment, Shelly was confused. "I might . . ." she rummaged in her toolbag for one, a couple seconds longer than her still-tense friend could handle.

He snapped his fingers. "It really can't wait. We don't have time."

Over Imtiaz's shoulder, Runako held a long looped black cable, its connectors seemingly brand new. "Don't bother. One right here."

"Thank you," Imtiaz said, snatching it from him, tossing one end of it to Shelly. She slid a panel to the side of the robot's head—one of the few parts of it still covered—and inserted it.

Imtiaz opened a command console and began his wizardry. He had learned a couple of tricks online ever since robots came in vogue, but they were light reading. He never anticipated actually having to apply them. There were never supposed to actually have any on his island. They were too expensive for leisure, save for the wealthiest corners of Cascade or Westmoorings where some fair-skinned grandfather with an Irish last name lived out his lonely retirement.

The government swore against them for public sector purposes, citing price mostly, but police bots were a particularly hot topic. They weren't just costly to most leaders. They were problematic—too much power for anyone in office to hold. Leaders of the opposition for the last few years milked that argument in the parliament house—"Do you want our Prime Minister having full rein over armed machines? With no consciences? Wandering our streets under the guise of law and order, but really, she's asking the people to pay for her own personal hit squad!" Another oft-milked idea—they called it the 'flying squad'—was a rumoured group of non-robotic policemen with a license to kill and a direct line to the Minister. Putting those two ideas together was a good way to whip up a panic.

But then again, here was proof of one of the claims being true. A police bot. Number and all. The first known sighting–if only they survived the night.

A couple lines of code later, a small window popped up–the bot's application screen. *Reboot Y/N?* He pressed the Y key, and another line of text appeared: *Rebooting* . . . They could hear a low whirring from the gears near the battery, and the robot's LED eyes began to slowly fade in and out in a bright blue.

"Hurry up, nah, you dotish robot," Imtiaz muttered. A sliver of him had all but given up that they would make it back out unnoticed with the robot in tow. But he had already begun. There was nothing left but to soldier on.

The robot's head slowly tilted up, and a gentle, melodious bootup theme played from its neck, a little louder now without some of the plating to muffle it. Shelly's hands shot up in triumph as she waited to hear it greet itself. The robot opened its dull-grey mouth and spoke:

"Çàðàâñòâóéòå. ß îìàåü Mèíåðàâ, ñåðèéíûé íîìåð TTPS-8103-X791. ß îîãó ÷àì-íèàóäü îíîî÷ü?"

"What?" Runako scratched his head. "What kinda language is that?"

"I don't know, boy." Shelly finished screwing the final plate, and then inched closer to Imtiaz. "Im, something wrong with the language options or what?"

"Maybe . . ." He went back into command prompt, typing in more code to get access to its folders. "But if it's a neural wiring problem–"

"I just looked at it, Im. Everything in order. Don't blame it on–"

"I not blaming anybody. I just saying we can't solve this now. Police all over. We have to take this home and troubleshoot it there."

"Nah. I can't wait. I need to be sure Runako not setting me up."

"Even if we make jail?" Imtiaz turned to her in panic.

Shelly pointed at his laptop screen. "Face front. If you don't want to make jail, work faster. We getting out of here, and we getting out of here with this robot."

Imtiaz rubbed his eyes anxiously before pressing the Enter key. There was a briefer, louder whir, and then the bot powered down, its folders spilling onto the screen in a small cascade. "Okay, the root is here . . ." He fished around for the language base. "Um . . . all I see here is Russian and Japanese. I can't even find its preferred warning phrases document." He put a few more lines in the command box to update its language files. "Okay, two minutes at least that's fixed. I'll have to reboot it again first."

"Alright, what about everything else? Optical recording? Ear-side microphones? The riot gear?"

Imtiaz squinted at the rest of files and folders. "They all look fine here. Due for updates, but they could run fine till we get back home. So?" He gestured sternly to the window? "Can we?"

"Make sure for me, please?"

At this point, he was sweating. He couldn't see through the window. At least seeing outside confirmed his fears. Now, worry just ran amok in his mind. He was sure he had just heard a gunshot higher up the street. He closed his eyes for a moment, took a breath, and then opened them again, scanning the filenames for anything missing. Instead, he found new ones.

"When you find this?" he said.

Runako shifted, rubbing his hand over the top of his shiny bald head. "Who, me? Like, some weeks. Why?"

He turned to Shelly, eyes wide, beads of sweat falling down his cheeks. "Because it still have recordings, Shell."

She straightened up, leaning closer to see the screen. A folder headed GATHER had reams of voice notes and video, most of which were so badly corrupted that their file types were missing, surely a result of whatever damage the bot had received. All of them were titled with numbers, and they had even more text files with the same kind of file name.

Shelly pointed to one at random, a text file. "Twelve oh nine, twenty twenty-three, sixteen thirty-four forty-one, oh thirty-nine? What that mean?"

"Most likely date and time, and . . . the last three, a place? Number of files on that day? I don't know." He opened it and read aloud. "'Event log, September 12th 2023'—wait, nah, that was just the other day?—'deployed on raid procedure in Arima area, address 34 Lime Avenue. Related files withheld by Winged Cpt. Sean Alexander.' It have the number of people in the house, outstanding warrant info . . . it says, 'Winged Det. Dexter Sandy, in compliance with Winged Cpt. Alexander, found previously tagged evidence 46859 in previously sealed case Trinidad & Tobago vs. Kareem Jones, which led to the arrest of—"

"Wait!" Runako stood behind Imtiaz, his hands pressed firmly on the back of the chair. "Previously tagged? You getting this, Shelly?"

"What? I don't follow." She hadn't turned to face either of them, still reading the file. Imtiaz stared at it with a mild confusion.

"That evidence! Kareem Jones was in the papers months now for weed possession. He already in jail! How would they find already-seized weed in Arima from a case in Carenage, on the west side?"

"And what is a 'winged' officer?" Shelly made scare-quotes with her fingers as she said it.

"I was wondering the same thing," Imtiaz said. "What kind of designation is that? It sure doesn't sound official."

"I could damn well tell you what it is—"

"I don't want to believe it . . ." Shelly turned back to the robot, as if taking it in. It wasn't just an illegal bot—it was a flying squad bot. A metal goon for the Prime Minister. It took a moment too long for Imtiaz to put it all together, but the moment he had, the back of his neck felt warm.

"It have video for that day here?" Runako put his hands on Imtiaz's shoulders—and it made him even tenser still.

"L-lemme see." He scrolled through them to find a video with the exact same title. He double-clicked it, and it loaded in his media player, a four-minute recording starting with the camera—the bot—leaving a police vehicle.

"Ey! Open up! Police!" A gruff man's voice shouted from outside of view. The bot looked directly at the door of an apple-white house as it slowly opened, a short brown girl looking out timidly.

"Where your parents, girl?" another, softer, male voice said, still in a raised voice. The girl shook her head in reply, stepping back into the house, but a heavy-set officer ran up to the door and held it open.

They could hear someone else shouting inside. The officer at the door, the gruff one, shouted, "Ey! We reach, so don't play like you're hiding nothing!" Two other officers came to the door and they entered, the robot behind them in the tight, dim walkway.

The robot glanced everywhere, and was making readings of everything. It tried to scan for the name of the girl, but couldn't find it; it calculated live on screen the percentage of threat posed by stray breadknives on the kitchen counter as they passed it, or of a cricket bat near the living-room window—low, it supposed, being sized for a primary school child, easy to deal with by a carbon-plated police bot.

It saw a man it identified at David Sellers, raising his voice at an officer, asking how they could barge into the house without a warrant.

It saw Sparkle Sellers, and brought up the recent date of

their marriage beneath her name as she pulled David back, trying to calm him down.

It saw an officer pull a bag as big as his palm out of his side pocket while no one was looking. It tagged the bag "E-46859", and followed awkwardly, focusing on it as the officer dropped it behind a plastic chair in the dining room. The officer nudged his partner and whispered, audibly enough for the robot, "It there, eh?" It saw him gesture with his elbow to the chair.

"What?" David shouted. "What where? What's going on here?"

"Sir, you are under arrest for possession of marijuana with intent to distribute," the gruff man said, reaching past Mrs. Sellers and grabbing David by his shoulder.

"Weed? You for *real*, officer? It have no weed here!"

He threw David on the brownish carpet, inches from the chair where they had dropped it, turning his head to face it as they put on the cuffs. "So what is that?"

The video stuttered here, playing that one moment repeatedly–of David Sellers' frightened gaze, fixed on the clear package on his floor, looping the very moment when his eyes widened with fear, and then relaxed again in sad resignation, over and over and over . . . .

For a moment, the three of them stared silently at the screen. Imtiaz's hands were on his mouth.

Suddenly, Runako and Imtiaz jumped in unison. There was a loud rapping at the outermost door.

"Shit," Runako whispered, beginning to pace in confused panic. "They catch we, fellas. That is it."

"Wait, stop freaking out, guys," Shelly said, getting up slowly.

Imtiaz still couldn't find the words. This was it. They were done. They had in front of them what was probably an illegally sourced repository of evidence of police impropriety in the house of a career criminal drug offender. They were done for.

"Okay," Shelly added. "We keeping the files, for sure."

"How we going to keep what we can't leave the house with?"

"Easy. We leave the house."

Imtiaz wanted to shout, if not for the fear of police. "How?"

"Boot up the bot. We flying out."

Runako started mumbling to himself. "We backing up everything. Four or five copies. And you going to take them. Don't get catch, eh?"

"Wait, no, stop—how this supposed to work?" Imtiaz put his hands out to Shelly. "This is nonsense. How we flying out with the robot? It can't even speak English yet!"

"It don't need to. It just need to be able to fly."

He checked the download—just complete. The flight module seemed to be fine in software, but he wasn't convinced that Shelly had it all worked out on the hardware end. He didn't like this idea at all. "Can we just think this over for—"

Outside, they heard someone tapping on the door. "Excuse me, this is the police—"

The three of them froze, their voice down to whispers. Imtiaz pointed at Shelly. "Okay, but let it be known I think this is craziness."

"Foolish is fine once it works—" She gripped the robot's left arm firmly, then leaned over to the keyboard to begin another reboot sequence. "You better had grab hold of something. Runako, you coming with us?"

"Nah. Somebody have to take the licks," he whispered. He was standing at the door now, facing it at attention. "Just get out quick."

Shelly nodded, then looked sternly at Imtiaz, who shot her a confused look. The moment the robot's boot sound sprung to life, he suddenly grabbed hold of its free arm.

"Hello," it said. "I am model Minerva, serial number TTPS-8103-X79I. How may I help you?"

"By getting airborne," Shelly whispered. "Uh . . . Hostiles en route, or whatever."

"Understood." Suddenly, its wings spread open with a tinny, rusty clang. Its edges hit both walls without even opening fully, and then it just as suddenly retracted them. "Wingspan obstacle issue." It turned to Shelly. "Primary launch will include thrusters only. Will that be a problem?"

"Nah, you do what you have to do, man." The moment Shelly said this was when Imtiaz realized he was about to do something well and truly foolish.

The knocking at the door became more insistent, and the officer's voice harsher. "You better open up right now before I have to kick this blasted—"

The bot's thrusters thrummed to life, warm air gushing from it. It turned to Imtiaz. "Please hold on to my arms with both hands. Flight may often be turbulent and dangerous."

"No shit—" Shelly nearly exclaimed it, but another persistent knock at the door brought her back to whispers. "We should go now, you know."

"Understood," the bot replied.

A louder, harder purr of wind and heat flooded out of the thrusters, and the bot sprang up with its two parcels on each side, through the galvanised sheet roof with enough force to push it clean off. They didn't have enough time to ready themselves; Imtiaz would have slid all the way off its arm if it hadn't swivelled its palm to grab his belt buckle. Shelly responded by wrapping her limbs around its arm for more support.

The robot spread its wings, and the thrusters let out an even harder gust. "Clearing distance. What is our destination?"

"Take me to San Juan," Shelly shouted into its microphoned ear.

"Understood." It flapped its chrome-feathered wings once, and then sped east with a force Imtiaz swore would tear his flesh from the rest of him.

Imtiaz looked down to see three police officers rush through the door, one of them already pinning Runako to the wall. Another reached for his pistol and let out one shot, narrowly missing the robot's forehead, and by extension, Imtiaz.

Shelly would later spring Runako from prison with the spoils of her newfound publicity. Runako's charge, again, was drug pushing, until the real news broke. Shelly sent a compact disc to every major television station as soon as she had watched all of the video herself—hours of video of 'winged' officers kicking in doors, windows, and the occasional civilian's face; dozens of false arrests and misappropriations, with all the officers' faces on screen. Imtiaz refused to look at them. They both spent their quiet moments trembling at the thought of what must have been on the videos that were lost to hard drive damage and time. The Prime Minister resigned two nights after, owning up to the whole flying squad programme. The new hot topic on the web, though, was that till the snap election was done, the citizens would be under a state of emergency anyway.

As for the bot, Shelly put it to work helping her mother around the house on her behalf. She had tinkered with it so intensively that it had taken to cooking their dinner and tending to their herb garden with near-mathematical accuracy. On weekends, she strapped a bespoke harness around its wings and learned to fly with it for fun, a hobby which frightened her mother every single time.

"What's next for the girl who blew the whistle on the Flying Squad fiasco?" the press would ask her every other day in the papers.

"Graduate from UWI?" she'd reply, shrugging, looking away from the cameras like she was already bored with it all.

Imtiaz managed to keep his face out of the papers, for his own sake. Even his husband had yet to hear of the drama of that night. He'd have the occasional paranoid episode coming from work, though, looking in his rearview mirror for flashing blue lights as he hurried down the highway. Whenever he found himself panicking, he raised the volume on his industrial-rock driving music just a little higher.

Imtiaz grew to enjoy the safety of his house. He held on to Tevin a little tighter every day. He'd even find himself grinning like a fool at the simplest, most mundane questions, simply because he was still around to answer them.

"Didn't have any problems getting back?" Tevin would ask.

"Nah," Imtiaz would reply. "Traffic was light today. You know how it is."

KEVIN JARED HOSEIN

Maiden of the Mud

Trinidad & Tobago

drive him mad whenever I can, just because I can. Me and him—
we have a connection. I ain't know how, but I could tell you—he
livin good-good over there and I dead as dead over here. It
must have some thread that hangin in-between, extendin from
my mouth and fastenin round his neck, cause when I speak the
man name—Leon—he and only he could hear. And it ain't take
long for him to start listenin. And he'd come in the night, drag-
gin he nice shoes along the muddy bank, smellin like rum, voice
tremblin like a schoolyard sissy.

He make sure to bring two gallon of milk with him every
time. See, is not only me who cryin out for him. Have a next one
here. A baby girl. A scrawny little thing. I never give the child no
name—never get the chance back then, and never bother to now.
The thing wasn't even born when I dead. I wake up here in Waterloo Bay, face-down in the mud, just a stone throw away from the
old pyres. And the child was right next to me, cryin, cryin. It was
wet, covered head to toe with muck and slime. I stare at it for a few
minutes, wonderin if it was a creature of foot or fin, lung or gill.

Had nothin I could do to ease the child. The child didn't want
my milk. The cries pierce the air like sirens—nothin you coulda
ever think come outta a baby mouth. When it first start, I didn't

know what to feel. Mostly, it was confusion. Then annoyance. Then rage. Lookin at it, its toothless mouth, oyster-grey skin, cheeks scrunched like soggy cotton, eyes small and shiny like soursop seeds, I coulda only think bout settin it to drift down at sea. It might pluck itself outta the lazy ebb and swim back to me, I know, but at least the place would have peace and quiet. Just for one night, oh God—quiet.

I was never this kinda woman, you know, not before I shack up with a guy name Shivan Sharma. I used to sing, mostly in hotels and weddings. I ain't never believe in the songs I sing, at least not after the paychecks start comin in less and less. I was lookin to get out. Where I meet Shivan was at his sister's wedding. I remember the decorations—red and gold everywhere. One thing that catch my eye was a big blown-up photo of the bride and groom, Lakshmi and Leon. The two figures, frozen midway in some dippin dance move, obscenely highlighted in a carousel of airbrush and bloom.

I remember thinkin: this Leon could be a model—every hair in place, neat scythe-shaped eyebrows, strong angular jaw, devilishly handsome grin. Lakshmi sheself—not so pretty. Thin lips, thick eyebrows, short stature, flat. Really not the kinda woman you gon expect to see with a man like Leon. It become apparent to me that Leon was the trophy, not she. See, that whole family was born in money—you know, them uppity, fair-skin, high-class Indians. So when Shivan wanted to have an after-party fling with the wedding singer, it make my blood crawl at first. Boys from these kinda families was accustom to gettin whatever they wanted and whoever they wanted. But I had to suck it up. He was my ticket outta this life of uncertainty. So I make sure to do the deed right. I stroke all the right spots, lick all the right parts, tell him how big and majestic his penis was—I make the boy fall in love. And well, before I know it, the boy bring me home to meet Mother Sharma.

But that old woman didn't like me at all, at all. She look for faults everywhere and fill them with salt. I try to cook lunch for the woman once and everything was missin something–the curry have no chadon beni, the rice have no cardamom, this thing need more vinegar, that thing need more pimento. But wasn't just that. It just start off that way. The next day, my hair lack volume. The day after, my skin need lightenin. Next day, my teeth need straightenin. I needed to fix my sour face, smile more, sit straight, tone up, moisturise, deep-cleanse, exfoliate. By the end of the first two months, I didn't have enough academic qualifications, didn't have enough distinctions, certificates, diplomas, accreditations. For this woman to stop harassin my tail, I needed a BSc, a BA, a LLB, a MFA, a PhD. Tell you, this old woman was drivin me mad! She used to deny it, though. If I ever bring it up, the old bitch would throw her arms up in the air and holler, "But I have *no* problem with you, dear, what a silly thing to say!"

Leon wasn't no scholar, and she never treat him like she treat me! But he did take notice of her behaviour. He say that he went through the same nancy-story. Was strange when he wanted to exchange numbers, but I went ahead. When he call, we would badtalk the Sharmas. He used to call them the Brahmins, which woulda make we the Dalits, the Dravidians, the Untouchables. We bond like that, jokin bout how we coulda eat at the same table with these Brahmins. One thing that stick out to me was when he tell me, "Is a while since I coulda laugh at something I actually find funny."

But no matter how much I talked with Leon, I ain't learn much. Might sound weird, but he was unknowable, secretive while appearin to be an open book. Have a way he curl his eyebrows when he talk–you know that the man hidin things. His honesty was an illusion and I suddenly had the notion that he was lyin in bed next to Lakshmi, tellin her all the things I used to say, bout all the vulgar badtalk comin outa my mouth. It coulda be a plot from Mother Sharma to get rid of me. Leon wasn't exactly the apple of the woman eye, but she still give him a chance in the textile business she was runnin. What Leon coulda know bout textiles?

As for me, well, I was useless. No room for me in that equation. The woman had no opportunities for me. She wanted me gone! Never had a day she wouldn't nag Shivan to get a girl who wasn't a damn wedding singer. Shivan used to ask me to sing for them—like a puppy trained to do tricks. Like the issue was the quality of my singing and not my career choice. He was a desperate boy, is all I could say. Desperate for mummy's approval.

"She's not going to one day be singing at the Metropolitan, darling," she used to say to Shivan. And one day, Lakshmi back it up with, "You sure she doesn't sing for funerals?"

That's what Leon told me. I didn't know what to say. I expected lines like that from the old, senile bitch, but not from Lakshmi. I barely ever talk to Lakshmi, but I was hurt. I have a thick skin, but that sting real bad. That night, I invite Leon over to my apartment. Was under the guise to go out and watch a movie. Lakshmi didn't like goin to the cinema—she was that kinda woman—so she was happy for Leon to find a movie-friend. I tell him to come up and wait for me. When he walk in the door, I was already naked on the couch. He waste no time—he jump on me and we went at it three times. He was of a different world from the Sharmas. A different creature. He didn't belong in whatever birdcage they was keepin him in.

I did it to get at Lakshmi and, by extension, Mother Sharma. I wanted to ruin the family. Was for no other reason, really. It feel good knowin that there was some things they had no control of. So I let the affair go on for bout a month. He tell me he was in love, he tell me I had perfect breasts, he tell me everything was different with me, how mechanical Lakshmi was and how organic I was—foolishness like that. He tell me he would leave his wife for me, but I ain't stupid—I know how men does talk. I never let it fool me, not for a minute. Leon was useless without his wife, anyway. I would never talk bout Shivan with him, though he insist I should. The only comparison I ever make was when I tell him, "You taste like him, but sweeter."

I let it go on until Shivan get rid of me. No, he ain't never find out bout the affair—he was as clueless as his sister. His mother end up gettin the best of him. The breakup was simple. One phone call, one last roll under the sheets, and I put my dress back on and went my way. I ain't beg for him. To tell you the truth, I was relieved—I didn't realize it until a few days after. My phone was filled with missed calls from Leon. But I never bother to call back until I wake up vomiting one mornin. So I did the test the next day—and yes, I was pregnant. Wasn't Shivan's—he always use protection. Leon didn't.

So I call up Leon and let him know what was goin on. He was quiet-quiet at first. Wouldn't be hard to imagine what was goin through his head, but you coulda never know with him. "I gon be there for the child," he tell me. "I know what is like to come into this world with nobody." But after that, all calls went unanswered. Texted constantly, no replies. Is hard to explain what it feel like—I was a fruit, ready to be juiced dry into some bitter cocktail. Blood and progesterone burned like shots of straight Scotch every mornin. Every step I take feel like an oar stroking a heavy arc of water. I thought bout gettin rid of the child, but that was a more frightenin thought than havin it. All I coulda think bout was metal and blades and scissors in a bright sterilized room. Surgery of the soul. I couldn't do it.

One day I left a voice message for Leon, tellin him that I'd tell his wife bout the baby if he don't reply. Was just a threat, just a lil somethin to stir the fear in him. Well, the phone ring, ring, ring! I coulda hear talkin and shufflin in the background and he

was whisperin to me, "You can't do this to me. I'll lose *everything.*
Do you know how much I sacrificed?"

But I kept up the threat, sayin, "Be a man and take responsibility, Leon. I have pictures of you in my apartment if you
don't." Actually, I didn't.

A week later, he called and asked to come over. He'd pick me
up and we'd drive and talk. So we drive down to Waterloo, near
the cremation site by the Temple in the Sea. Well, Leon ain't
come to talk that night. He cut the lights, lean over and press his
thumbs against my neck.

Stranglin me right there in the passenger seat.

His eyes was watery and red. He was snarlin like a dog.

I couldn't breathe, couldn't kick him offa me.

I stretch my arm to open the door.

It fly open and I fall backward, my head upside-down, his
thumbs still jam against my throat. A colony of dogs in the distance lift their eyes at me. No sound but the muted rumble from
the water, sloshing salt into the wind. The moonlight falling on
the queue of jhandi flags poking out from the mud. A small boat,
anchored to a bamboo pole, bobbed silently in the bay.

I saw these things as the light was bein squeezed outta me.

Couldn't remember nothin else.

When I wake up, I was face-down in the silt. I still can't an-
gle my neck straight—it have a perpetual crook in it. My clothes
was drenched and bloody round the waist. And a baby was next
to me, cryin, cryin, cryin. I ain't even realize I was dead at first—
me and this baby that was inside of me. Nobody coulda see me,
nobody coulda see the child. I was shock at first. I underestimate
Leon! Didn't think the man had it in him! Ain't nobody gon look
for me, ain't nobody in this world to miss me. It probably ain't
even had a body to find. Just one more woman fall off the Earth—
dispensable flesh.

Leon didn't start comin to see me till a full month later. I ain't know how else to put it—but he look like *shit*. I ain't think it was guilt, but I still could never be sure. Death ain't have no clarity to it, you know. It more confusin than life. Lookin at life from the outside make me miss it. Ghosts couldn't have company unless they haunt somebody. So as I say before, I drive him mad whenever I could, just because I could. The first time he drive down here and see me standin near the flags, my clothes tattered, my pale bloated skin drippin wet, he just drop to his knees. He ain't try to run. He ain't scream or bawl.

All I coulda say to him was, "The child want milk, Leon."

So whenever he come, he make sure to bring two gallon of milk, because this child always hungry! He *have* to bring it, because I find out something I coulda do. I coulda yank the lives of babies right from the womb. I do it to a woman who was starin out at the sunset here near the temple. Rip the baby's soul right outta she and watch the blood spill down her dress and legs.

It was *incredible!*

Now, at the time, Lakshmi was pregnant. Don't ask me how I know—I just know. The dead know these things. I didn't even have to be near she. I let Leon know what I would do if he ever stop comin. I would tear that baby right outta she and I would belt out a wedding song for the fuckin funeral!

This went on for months. Had a time he lie against my breast and tell me bout his father—walk right outta his life before he was born—like I could care. He tell me this child mean everything to him. Every time he come, he'd snivel and beg me not to take his child—that it was the only good thing in his life. I tell myself I woulda keep stringin him along and kill the baby at the eighth month. But the joke was on me; the baby was born premature at seven months. A healthy, pink, flushed baby boy. Unfortunately.

Suddenly, I had no authority over it, but I didn't let Leon know that. I let him believe I coulda still snatch it away from him at any time. I enjoy it for a while, but it get boring. Just one day, I decide to let Leon go. He seem unhappy enough with his life. His marriage makes him suffer worse than I did. I try luring some other men into the water, but I tell you—it get boring.

Round that time, had a few folks that start sensin somethin was goin on at the bay. Maybe they coulda feel me breathin down their neck, or hear me callin out to them. Maybe they coulda see the splashes in the water that I make. Or maybe I abort one too many foetuses near the temple. I dunno—I lost count long time. They give me all kinda names—churile, jumbie girl—but the one I like the most was *maiden of the mud*, probably because they start seein the footprints I leave whenever I walk cross the silt. Maiden remind me of how young I was. I wasn't no hag or no witch. I was a maiden.

You know, I'm not so much a ghost, I'm a demon. A young demon. And I feel like demons ain't born. Demons are made. Demons are moulded. Demons get stuck wanderin a place over and over for centuries, hauntin the same old people, unable to move forward with time. Women demons, especially, obsess with man and only man. Why? This is how I want eternity to play out? Hauntin some string of men? Listenin to some child cry whole day? Even in death, I realise I still stuck bein a blasted untouchable.

Must have somethin better out there, I keep thinkin. So today, I get up and leave the child to cry. Funny how I never think to just leave it behind before. In death, decisions like that don't even come to mind normally. The farther I walk away from it, the softer the cries get. Until it dwindles into silence. Peace and quiet, at last.

I turn round and see the child has always been nothin but a stone. I turn round and head back to see if the light been playin tricks on me. But no, it right there, just a big chunk of rock. Has it just been playin a prank on me and Leon the whole time? I dunno. I could never know. I hold it in my arms now. I drop it into the ocean and watch it dissolve into a flurry of black ribbons.

In the distance, bands of clumpy grey clouds swell and taper cross the sky, the dust-coloured twilight shootin out through the cracks. But the cracks soon stitch up and the darkness stretches cross the sea. The iron gloom is mantled with a twisted matrix of lightning. The temple standin still at the end of the stone jetty; the tides startin to lash against concrete.

I squint my eyes and peer at the slow swirl of clouds. A giant plume of rain blowin in from the rumblin horizon. A storm comin. It tellin me, Girl, you have to go. It tellin me, Girl, it's time to move on. It tellin me, Girl, you free to leave this place.

RICHARD B. LYNCH

Water Under the Bridge

Barbados

Janice looked down at the water under the swing bridge and stared at her reflection. Even at a distance, she could see the fear on her face. She was scared because it was Friday. Friday was scary since her mother started to work the graveyard shift at the gas station and she was left in the care of her mother's boyfriend.

Janice would ask her mother not to go to work but her mother always answered, "I have to, li'l girl." Janice would ask if she could stay with her mother's sister, but her mother always answered, "Don't confuse me, chile."

It was about three months ago when the boyfriend came to live with them. At first he spent most of his time in the bedroom with Janice's mother, but gradually spent more time just loafing around the house. Janice would come home from school and find him in the small living room in front of the television with her mother—in each other's arms. She felt that her mother was ignoring her.

Sometimes, after school, Janice would sit with them while they watched television. Then, everything was pretty all right, but one time when her mother went to the kitchen, Janice caught the boyfriend staring at her. She felt frozen under his stare. She occasionally glanced in his direction, hoping he would be looking away, but he only removed his eyes when her mother returned to the room. Janice tried to tell her mother about the incident the next morning, but her mother told her that the boyfriend was probably just high.

The first evening that her mother worked the graveyard shift, the boyfriend just sat and watched television while Janice read her books in her room. It was on the third or maybe the fourth time they were alone when he invited Janice to sit on the sofa with him. That night he put on a good action flick, which Janice enjoyed.

The next time he called her to watch a movie with him, she did not enjoy it. The movie was about people kissing and being in bed with each other and doing "lovey dovey," as her friends at school would say. The next time they watched a movie together, Janice knew they were watching a blue movie. She had heard the boys at school talking about them—about whose father had the most. She sat through it, stiff as a plastic doll, grateful when it came to an end. Then he sent her to bed.

Janice told her mother about the movie and her mother confronted the boyfriend about it. He sucked his teeth and said, "Is either she imagination, or she trying to get me in trouble. We watch a movie and it might-uh had in some kissing and ting but I wuh never put on a blue movie in front you chile."

Janice's mother flogged her that night and told her not to "mess up tings" with her and her man. After that, on Friday nights, the boyfriend continued to call Janice to watch movies. Sometimes he even dragged her out of her room to make her watch. It was not always pornography, but he made her sit on his lap, whispering in her ear as he touched her. "You muhduh ain't eva gine believe you, cause she like dis same touch too much. Don't scream, hear, cause I wuh break you neck right hey."

Janice cringed as she sat on his lap. She looked at the television, thinking that this was what got her in trouble in the first place. She looked at the linen cupboard and wished she was inside it and away from this man. She looked at the picture of Jesus with his hands outstretched, and wished he would come off the wall to help her.

Now, looking down at her reflection in the water under the swing bridge, she recalled her conversation with the old woman who sold tamarind balls outside school. In truth, the old woman had spoken to her.

She looked into Janice's eyes and said, "You troubled, li'l girl chile. Wha' troubling you?" Janice just stood there, looking back at the old lady. The next day was Friday, but Janice was afraid this woman would react as her mother had.

"*Who* troubling you is de real question?" the old woman said. "It is time yuh help yuhself. Do exactly as I tell you."

Janice pulled a jar from her bag and carefully reached into her pocket for the egg she had stolen from the supermarket across the street. She had been very careful not to bump into anyone while leaving, so as to protect the egg. She slid an egg into the jar, easing in her fingers as far as she could so it wouldn't break, screwed the lid back onto the jar and let it drop from the swing bridge. The jar broke her reflection as it hit the water. When the reflection reformed, instead of fear, she now could see hope.

When Janice got home she was shocked by what she saw, even though the old woman had prepared her well. The television was on, and sitting in front of it on the sofa in the small living room was a little girl. From behind, Janice could see that the little girl's hair was in the same style as her own. She crept over to the sofa and stared wide-eyed. The face was a perfect reflection of her own.

She remembered the old woman's instructions: "Don't look at she long, cause she gine see dat you is she and she gine leff. Just find someplace good to hide."

Janice opened the linen cupboard and pulled out a few things from the inside, spilling them onto the floor. She crawled into the space and closed the door behind her. Janice could see what was in the living room through the slats of the cupboard doors.

Janice's mother came out of her bedroom, ready for work. "Janice! I hope you plan to tek up all dese tings you got pun de floor." She saw what they were and shouted. "Janice, how you cuh tek out my tings and just leff dem dey! I gine work and tings better not be so in de morning when I get home!"

Janice's mother called to her boyfriend. "I leffing hey now. Mek sure dis chile clean up dis mess." Janice stayed in the cupboard, waiting, feeling sick that she was leaving this other child to face her horrors. She almost burst out from her hiding spot to tell the other girl to leave, but the boyfriend walked into the room. Janice could see his naked legs and she knew that he was wearing nothing but boxer shorts.

"Wait!" he cooed. "I surprise I ain't had to call yuh out. Yuh starting to like wha' yuh getting, nuh?" The little girl on the sofa did not move. She was out of Janice's vision when the boyfriend sat between them. Janice could tell that he was looking into the girl's eyes, because he always looked into her eyes before he told her to sit on him.

But this time he did not tell her to sit on his lap. He did not say anything as he sat next to the impostor. She had taken his voice! Janice did not know the extent of the impostor's powers but she felt certain it was exerting them now. Her double looked deeply into the boyfriend's eyes and seemed to know his intentions. He, looking back, must have seen hers. He trembled but he did not move. When he tried to speak, a click-clicking sound seemed to come from his throat.

Janice sat wondering what would happen next.

The boyfriend spun his head, looking towards the linen cupboard. Janice whimpered in surprise. His arms were flailing and thrashing. His lips were peeled back and his mouth and eyes were opened wide as he tried to scream. Still, under the double's power, nothing came out.

"Dah's how I does feel," she whispered as fear gave way to satisfaction. It was difficult to see what was going on, but Janice could see the boyfriend struggling, as if trying to get away from the sofa, but being restrained, pulled back. Janice saw what looked like a very long tongue slide from under the boyfriend, who was now on his belly, still trying to get off the sofa. The tongue licked his face, and his mouth opened wider, tears running down his cheeks, but still with no sound coming out. Janice stopped looking, remembering the old woman's words.

"De baku gine consume yuh troubles," she had said. "When it done, just come out and look at it. It gine see dah it is *you* it imposturing. And den it gine leff. But it ain't gine leff you till it consume all yuh troubles."

When Janice opened her eyes, she could see the double in the same position she was in before the boyfriend walked in. The boyfriend was gone. Janice could see just his boxer shorts on the floor and she knew that he was gone forever. If only her mother had believed her, none of this would have happened.

Janice started to open the cupboard door, but fear still gripped her. She reminded herself that she could trust the old woman. Then she remembered that she still had one more problem and she tucked herself further into the linen cupboard, to make herself more comfortable. It would be a long wait in this cubbyhole till her mother got home.

ELIZABETH J. JONES

The Ceremony
Bermuda

Maggie hated her daughter on sight. The moment the nurse placed the tiny, dark haired baby in her arms, she took one look at it and turned her head away. The delivery hadn't been that painful—far easier than the one she had experienced with her first, her son, Frederick, as her husband Thomas pointed out. But Frederick's birth had been such a, such a *relief.* Because he wasn't a girl. His eyes had been different—they had looked into hers with a blind trust. This newborn's eyes pierced into Maggie's psyche as if to say: "It's not about you, you know—it's about me. And it always will be."

Maggie couldn't tell Thomas what she saw in the babe's eyes—but she couldn't hold the child either.

"Your pregnancy this time round was harder," Thomas had said sympathetically at her bedside, holding the infant against his chest and looking absolutely besotted. "You were so sick for so long and so tired. No wonder you're too exhausted to hold her. Now, what are we going to call her?"

"Don't be a damn fool, Thomas! What choice do we have in the matter? We can't call it after *your* mother, can we? It has to be Christabel, Christabel, Christabel."

He hadn't argued then, in deference to what he saw as her

exhaustion. But later he tried while they were waiting for her mother in the drawing room of the main house.

"She doesn't have to be named after your mother, you know. She doesn't have to be Christabel. Not if you give up the estate. It's not as if I don't have any money or property. My apartment is bigger than the whole of this, let alone the "Daughter's Domain", and it's in much better condition."

"I can't give up the estate, Thomas, you know that. It has been in my family for centuries and as the oldest daughter, it's my responsibility . . ."

"More like a burden. A crumbling ruin."

"It's the *land*, Thomas. Who else in Bermuda has fifty acres of unspoiled land? If I give it up, it goes to the Government. That's the rule of the entailment."

Thomas shrugged. "Why not let the Government have it? They could turn it into a park. It would be fairer on Frederick. It would be fairer on the whole of Bermuda. Let's face it, this is the last bastion of white privilege. It's not everybody who gets to enjoy this land. If it were a park, everybody would get to enjoy it."

Maggie looked through the double windows Grandmama Catherine had quaintly called French, though she had never been to France in her life, and took in the long familiar view, the rows of sago palms each side of the many steps leading down to the orange groves, the jacaranda trees, the fragrant frangipani, and eventually the long strip of beach. In the distance she could just see her family's constant enemies—the topless towers of Ilium as Catherine had called them after some quote in a weird old play—the gigantic sterile skyscrapers that made up the rest of Bermuda, circling, *menacing* her estate.

She shook her head violently. "No, no. I can't do that. The Government is dying to get its hands on it. Think of all the skyscrapers they could put up, the money involved. They'd never turn it into a park. And Grandmama Catherine would turn in her grave."

We can't let those monstrosities win, darling, Grandmama had said to her when she had been just a bitty little thing, running alone over the property, carefree and mindless of the concrete towers invading nearer and nearer. *Even if we have to make an enormous sacrifice. Remember that, dearest, whatever you do, because one day you will inherit,* you *will be the chatelaine.*

"If that's what you want," Thomas said.

"It's not what I want," she said, "but it's what I have to do."

So they named the child Christabel as the rules of inheritance required, but called her Bella to distinguish her from her beautiful grandmother who, with her violet eyes and cascading black hair, at sixty-seven didn't even look forty-seven. Maggie tried to put her first reaction to Bella's birth down to a bout of postpartum blues, although she knew that was not the case. Bella was by no means an ugly baby and yet she filled Maggie with revulsion. Ashamed, she made herself pick Bella up, cuddle her, carry out all the nurturing acts of love and kindnesses any natural mother would want to do, and that in the end might just be the saving of them both. But it was so difficult, although nobody, not even Thomas once the naming issue was decided, seemed to notice the enormous struggle it cost her. Nobody, that is, other than Bella, whose expression as she grew older became so sly and insolent whenever she set eyes on her mother, it took every ounce of Maggie's self-restraint not to smack her face. *Is* she as bad as I think, Maggie agonised, or is she just this way with me, reacting to my deepest fears?

By the time Bella was five, she was mistress of divide and rule. To Thomas, with her shining hair and her sweetest smile, she was a beloved and beautiful princess, incapable of an unkind thought. To Christabel, she was a joy, the shining light of the family's future. Grandma Christabel and Bella became so close scarcely a day went by without them seeing each other. But to Maggie, while they were alone together, she was quite simply obnoxious. When Maggie's friends told her about the sweetness of their daughters, the closeness they enjoyed with them, her heart felt heavy with terror and dread, because deep down she knew her daughter was cursed, just as she Maggie was cursed. In the future, there could be just one way out.

In contrast, Frederick, five years older, was a joyous child—he had the sweetness of his father, the same carefree, light-hearted nature. Maggie wasn't sure about his relationship with his sister, although he was always boisterously affectionate towards her, until one day, when he was ten, she overheard Bella's confident voice talking to him in one of the walled gardens, fringed with palmetto and mother-in-law's tongue. "This will be my garden, you know, and then you'll only be able to play in it if you do what I tell you!"

Maggie strode into the garden, ready to grab Bella. Then she stopped herself. I mustn't show my anger, she told herself. It will only give her more power.

"You okay, guys?" Her voice sounded forcedly cheerful to her own ears, but Frederick didn't seem to notice. He grinned at her, seemingly untouched by Bella's revelation.

"I'm fine. Can I go now? Dad says I can help with the bonfire."

And he was off, with Bella about to follow him.

"I need to talk to you, Bella. Please wait a minute."

Bella turned to her mother. "Yes?" She was never disobedient. It would be easier if she were—more normal somehow. She's so, so *condescending*.

"Bella," she said calmly, though her brain was seething, "who told you the garden will be yours one day?"

Bella smiled that sweet, sweet smile. "Grandma Christabel, she told me."

"Then she will have told you that before the land comes to you, it comes to me."

Bella smiled again, her green eyes so sly, so knowing. "Oh yes, she told me."

"So it's likely it won't come to you for a very, very, very long time. And that means Frederick can be in the gardens whenever he wants, do you understand me?"

Bella said nothing.

"*Do* you, Bella?"

"Grandma Christabel says it might not be a very, *very* long time."

"Oh really?"

Bella lowered her eyelids until her eyes were like slits. "Because of the *ceremony*," she said.

Maggie froze in shock. "What ceremony?"

"Grandma Christabel says you know all about it. But maybe you need to be reminded. That's what she says. Can I go now?"

"Well, maybe you do need to be reminded," said Christabel when Maggie remonstrated. "You were there, weren't you? When I came to the main house to claim my inheritance. You were there?"

Christabel had forbidden Maggie to be anywhere in Grandmama's garden that day, so of course Maggie's thirteen-year old just-say-anything-to-me-and-I'll-do-the-opposite psyche kicked in and she'd hidden behind one of the bushier sago palms.

Mama came so close walking past her, Maggie could have touched her long, tiered gypsy skirt grazing the steps as she approached the front door. She was still beautiful, gleaming black hair down her back, her eyes almost triangular, disturbingly violet. But Maggie, her eyes as usual cutting Christabel to pieces this way and that, to see if she could possibly compare, was glad to see the lines starting around her eyes, around her mouth. For once, Maggie felt she had an advantage. Awkward, clumsy she might be, but at least she wasn't *old*.

Then she heard the gravel crunch at the bottom of the steps and the alarm that announced the arrival of a vehicle. As Mama continued up the steps, Grandmama Catherine opened the door.

"Good morning, Christabel," she said.

The tone of her voice sounded odd to Maggie, who was holding herself behind the palm as tightly as she could. Was it fear?

"Good morning, Mama. I believe I heard Nathaniel arrive in his car."

Nathaniel Hayward? The family lawyer? What do they want him for, Maggie wondered. The only time she ever saw him was when he was a thin, tight-lipped presence at family cocktail parties. A pompous bore, mama had called him. "That man was born old, I swear," she said. But she always invited him to the family gatherings.

Christabel turned to greet Mr. Hayward as he climbed the steps. Maggie started to giggle. Her eyes took in a morning coat she had once seen in a family wedding photograph taken centuries ago. *He's wearing fancy dress! Why he's even wearing a top hat!* But then, as he passed inches by her, she could see the waxen pallor of his face and his expression was so funereal, she felt chilled to the bone, even though the air was dripping heat. She could see he was carrying a small wooden chest with a handle. What was he doing here?

The three figures went through the door and shut it behind them. Maggie leapt up the steps and tried to open the door, forgetting her image would be imprinted on the security system. That was the rule—if the door was open, she could come in whenever she wanted to but if it was closed, then Grandmama must not be disturbed. "If you try the door," Christabel had told her, "you will be seen and Grandmama will be cross."

But that day Maggie would not be put off. She skirted the

outside of the house, scratching her legs against the bougainvillea and plumbago bushes. Against the screech of the kiskadees, she could just hear Mr. Hayward's monotone coming from the window of the little Green Parlour on the ground floor that was never, never used.

She crouched under the stone lintel of the window so that she could peer in, hoping no one could see her. The walls of the parlour were an unusual pale avocado green, unusual because Grandmama's other rooms were all painted white. An old, old table of shining wood rested against the wall with nothing on it but a silver tray on which were placed two crystal glasses and two crystal decanters, one filled with a clear fluid, the other with a deep green liquid. The table reminded Maggie of an altar in a quaint old church. Mr Hayward, his top hat gone, stood by the table. Maggie watched him pour the clear liquid into one glass, the green into the other. He started to speak a strange language she'd never heard before. It's not Portuguese, she thought. Maybe it's that dead language Grandmama said she had to learn when she was little. Latin or something. Her eyes swivelled to Grandmama sitting taut and upright in one green velvet armchair, Mama smiling opposite her in the matching seat.

Mr. Hayward's voice suddenly grew louder. He switched to English. "Catherine Maria Waring, as it is set down by Henry Waring, your father, in his last will and testament, for the sake of your estate's longevity and safekeeping, do you promise to bestow twenty years . . ." His voice trailed off and she could not hear the rest of it.

Her mama's voice clear as a bell said sharply: "Mama?"

And then Maggie heard Grandmama Catherine's faltering tone, "I do."

He handed Grandmama the clear glass, Mama the green. Mama drank deeply, smiling all the while. Grandmama took a long breath.

"However difficult this is for you, Catherine," Mr Hayward was saying, "I'm sure you'll agree that it is in the best interests of the estate."

Grandmama nodded briefly, then slowly drained the glass.

It must be some kind of medicine, Maggie thought. It must taste disgusting. That's why poor Grandmama looks so fearful. But why is Mr. Hayward giving it to her? Why not the doctor and what is it for?

Mr. Hayward gravely returned to the table. He picked up the decanters and put them in the chest he had carried to the house. "I will be in touch, Christabel," he said softly. Then he left the room without saying anything to Grandmama. He didn't even glance at her.

Maggie heard the click of the parlour door. She dashed back to her hiding place behind the sago palm in time to see him come out of the front door, the chest hanging from his hand, and make his way down the steps. She wasn't sure what to do next. Go home and see if Mama would say anything? Wait and see if Grandmama would leave the door open so that she could visit? Just as she was pondering her options, Christabel appeared and skipped down the steps. She looks different, Maggie thought. Lighter somehow. Then Christabel stared directly at the hedge. Maggie gasped. There wasn't a line on her mama's face! Not one. She looked twenty years younger. And she knew, she knew Maggie had disobeyed her. Christabel paused deliberately for a full moment, flaunting herself in front of Maggie, and then continued down the steps. The words echoed in Maggie's head: . . . *for the sake of your estate's longevity and safekeeping do you promise to bestow twenty years . . . ?*

Her heart thudded with fear for her grandmama. What had she drunk from that glass?

Maggie turned back to the house. The door was open. She raced up to it, calling out to her grandmother. No answer. She ran inside, along the hallway to the Green Parlour, and flung open the door. Her face hidden, Grandmama Catherine was hunched in the green velvet armchair. *What has happened to Grandmama, she looks so* tiny, *and her arms and legs are so thin her dress could fall off!*

"Grandmama?"

Slowly, Grandmama raised her head. "Maggie?"

Maggie took one look and screamed.

"It's all right, Maggie, dearest, it's all right, I promise you."

Maggie's breathing was so fast she could hardly get the words out.

"You look so, so *old*. What's happened to you? Are you going to die, Grandmama?"

"Not yet, my darling. I'm going to teach you a little Latin first, dearest. When you are desperate, it could be the saving of you."

"You were there," Christabel said again as they sat at the old-fashioned round teak table in the little garden underneath The Green Parlour, inhaling the scent of the white Easter lilies, "weren't you?"

"You know damned well I was there. You wanted me to see it. And that was a terrible thing for a mother to do to her daughter."

Christabel smiled, the resemblance between her and Bella startling for all the difference in their eye colouring. "You had to know some time, Maggie."

"Why didn't you tell me?"

"It wasn't my place to tell you. After all, it was never expected of me, just as it won't be expected of Bella. But it is your sacred duty, as it was my mama's all those years ago."

"Supposing I don't do it? Supposing I don't give a damn about the land?"

"But you do give a damn about the land. Your grandmother made sure of that."

"Don't be too sure, Mama."

"I wasn't sure for a time. You seemed so happy with Frederick. But you went ahead and had a daughter, didn't you? And you called her Christabel."

"I did," Maggie said, willing her voice to sound even. "But that doesn't mean I'll agree to give her . . ."

"Oh, Maggie. It's far too soon for you to think about it now. When you're in your sixties, you'll feel differently about it."

"Technically, you are in your sixties now. How would you feel if I asked you . . . ?"

Christabel shrugged comfortably. "That's not the point, Maggie, is it? That's not the way the entailment goes."

"But shouldn't it be the point, Mama? What kind of daughter were you to ask Grandmother for such a sacrifice? And what kind of mother are you to expect it of me?"

"I am a grandmother, too, Maggie."

"Yes. You should think about that. What grandmother encourages her granddaughter to become a monster?"

Christabel shook her head. "A monster, Maggie? *Look . . .*"

Bella was slowly making her way from the side door of the house with a tray almost too heavy for her to carry. It had on it a glass jug of lemonade and two glasses. Painstakingly, she stepped towards their table.

"I made it, Grandma, I made it from the lemons in the garden. I made it all by myself."

"*Bella*, darling," cooed Christabel, "how sweet of you."

"Does it matter, Bella," said Maggie, "which glass is which?"

Maggie painfully tottered towards the double windows. Grandmama Catherine called them French, she thought. So sad, because I'm sure she never went to France in her life. She gazed out of them, taking in the so familiar rows of sago palms, the one behind which she had hidden all those years ago, and the long line of steps, broken at the edges. Then she turned back from the windows, limped into her chamber, her ankles and hips crippled with arthritis, and thought about the little Green Parlour.

So you are coming, Bella, thought Maggie, as she hobbled to the front entrance of the house. You are forty-six, of course, you are coming. And you will ask, won't you, what I knew you would eventually ask the moment you were born. You will ask what your grandmother asked, though it didn't do her much good. She died when you were just ten years old. I wonder if you ever thought about that, Bella?

Maggie watched Bella ascend the steps. Bella's skirt was not long. It hugged her excellent knees, showed off her shapely, toned legs. But her smiling expression? It's the same, thought Maggie, it's the same as Mama's was when I was there behind the sago palm. It's exactly the same. As a mother, I have failed you as much as Grandmama failed Mama. Monsters, both of you. I couldn't change you. What would Thomas think of you now, Bella, obsessed as you are with your right to the property?

Maggie shut her eyes, summoning Thomas's image before her. His hair was wild and tawny, his eyes alive and adventurous. Land had never mattered to him, just as it had not to his ancestors, although like many Bermudians of the time, they had acquired it through trading at sea. Long ago on sloops and schooners, they had roamed the ocean when it was untamed by the rigged edifices that stretched across the Atlantic and Pacific. A few centuries later they took to space instead and Thomas followed their spaceway path. That was one reason Maggie had been so attracted to him, even though she was as earthbound as he was tied to the firmaments. A patch of subtropical jungle in the middle of an urban wilderness could never have tamed him; she had always understood that. Besides, he was egalitarian in a way her family had never been.

His voice came echoing back over the thirty-nine year divide since he had disappeared in his space cruiser with Frederick on one of those damn fool trips he would take when he was bored.

"It's because of your mother, Maggs, it's because of Christabel, you don't have enough confidence in your looks."

"Well, Mama's beautiful!"

"Maybe. Everyone says so. But she acts like she's entitled and I don't find that attractive somehow. Your whole family acts like it's entitled. You're the only one that doesn't."

Dear Thomas. Yet he'd never seen through Bella. If I'd told him about the ceremony, Maggie thought, it might have been different. But how could I have done?

She made her eyes focus on the steps. There was Bella, climbing, climbing.

"Good morning, Bella," Maggie said. And prayed her voice did not sound frightened.

"Good morning, Mama," said Bella as she stood at the entrance.

Maggie heard the crunch of gravel and the alarm announcing a vehicle. Nathaniel is arriving, she thought. She watched him approach the steps. God, he's so old, so old. *Such a pompous bore*, she heard Christabel saying. There he was, in the morning dress she remembered, top-hatted and chest in hand.

And *there* coming up the steps as fast as her little legs could carry her was Lyla. The love of my life, thought Maggie. The one who will change everything, I'll make sure of that.

"Can I come in, Ga Ma?"

"Of *course*, you can, dearest."

"It's not suitable," Bella said sharply. "Go home, Lyla. Now."

Maggie held Lyla firmly in her arms.

"Good morning," said Nathaniel, arriving at the top of the steps. "Shall we begin?"

Once they were in the Green Parlour, he removed his hat, took out the two decanters and glasses from the chest and placed them upon the silver tray.

"It is, as I have explained to you, customary for the will of Henry Waring to be read in its entirety."

"Is that really necessary, Nathaniel?" Bella asked sweetly. "It's in Latin! Besides, you explained the terms of the will to me when I was twenty-one. And Mama knows them very well, don't you, Mama?"

Maggie nodded.

"Nevertheless," said Nathaniel in his deadly monotone, "It is important to follow the requirements to the letter, do you not agree, Maggie."

"I do."

He looked at Lyla, her little hand tucked into Maggie's. "I don't think it suitable for your granddaughter to remain, Maggie. It will be upsetting for her."

"At that point in the ceremony, she may leave," Maggie said, sitting down in one of the green velvet chairs and pulling Lyla onto her lap.

"As you wish, Maggie." He gestured to Bella who gracefully sat down in the other chair opposite.

He began to chant out the ten-page will and testament, his words dropping into the steamy air like incantations from a Latin mass.

Maggie saw Bella smiling, gazing steadily at the decanters on the silver tray, her green eyes as focused and as deadly as a cat's. Unable to bear the vision of her daughter, Maggie let her thoughts wander back to the day Bella was born, to Thomas's delight and her own despair.

I couldn't tell you, Thomas, I just couldn't tell you. You never understood about the land, did you? You would never have seen that sacrifice is necessary. You would never have forgiven me. And now, I couldn't blame you for it. When Frederick was born I was so happy, so very happy. But the pressure for a daughter was too great. I was trapped, Thomas, you have to understand that.

I thought there was no way out. And then I remembered what Grandmama had said to me the day of the ceremony I never told you about. *I'm going to teach you a little Latin, dearest. When you are desperate, it could be the saving of you!*

Nathaniel's reading came to a stop. He turned to the decanters, poured the green liquid from one into Bella's glass. Then he poured the clear fluid from the other into the glass that Maggie knew would be hers.

So I did learn Latin, Thomas, enough to understand everything in the will. The estate has to go down the female line; every other generation the daughter must be named Christabel. I told you that. But there are two other conditions, Thomas . . .

Nathaniel handed the green glass to Bella who tenderly cupped her long, tapered fingers around it.

It's a kind of spell, Thomas, a curse. Every Christabel Waring has the right to require her mother to give twenty years of her youth to her. If the mother refuses, after her death the land is sold to the Government, unless, unless . . .

Nathaniel solemnly gave the clear glass to Maggie.

"Can I have some, Ga Ma?" Lyla whispered.

"No, sweetheart," Maggie whispered back. "It's a nasty medicine you really don't need."

Nathaniel stood gravely by the table, then started to speak. "Margaret Maria Waring, as it is set down by Henry Waring, your great grandfather, in his last will and testament, for the sake of your estate's longevity and safekeeping do you promise to bestow twenty years of your life to your daughter, Christabel Maria Waring?"

Unless, Thomas, the child is the issue of a male Waring, in which case . . .

"Mama?" Bella's voice prodded her. "We're waiting."

"Oh," said Maggie, dryly, "I'd do anything for the estate, you all know that."

So, Thomas, when you were off on one of your space cruises, I went to Cousin Samuel, got him drunk, which wasn't hard to do . . . All the Waring men are drunkards—no wonder Henry Waring made that will. We had sex—Samuel was so smashed, he didn't remember a thing about it the morning after. But I got pregnant with Bella. Thank God, you never suspected a thing. Nobody did, because I was so in love with you.

"Maggie," said Nathaniel, "A simple 'I do' will suffice."

I figured, Thomas, that the only way it would matter would be if Bella asked me for her twenty years. A loving daughter would never ask for such a sacrifice, would she?

"Mama?" said Bella. "We're waiting."

"I do," said Maggie. "Now we are waiting for you, Bella. Aren't you going to drink?"

Bella drank the green liquid from her glass in one long swallow.

"My turn," said Maggie cheerfully and she drained her glass. Already her body felt lighter, her joints less swollen.

You see, Thomas, old Henry Waring despised the male Warings so much, he added a clause to the will. It's buried in the Latin verbiage but it's there. If a Christabel Waring is the issue of a male Waring and if she participates in the inheritance ceremony—*then* the spell is reversed.

Setting Lyla down, Maggie sprang lightly from her chair. "Come Lyla, it's time for you to play in the garden." She nodded slightly to Nathaniel, whose normally impassive face was so shocked she could have laughed. "Thank you, Nathaniel."

Maggie opened the front door and stood for a moment gazing down at the lawns and the gardens, at the strip of shoreline in the distance. In her mind she saw children running freely as she had run but they would not be generations of Warings—they would be of all colours, of all backgrounds. The park would belong to everyone. She smiled to herself as she imagined what Nathaniel would have to say about that.

Holding Lyla firmly by the hand, and skipping lightly down the steps, Maggie Waring left her daughter to her fate.

DAMION WILSON

Daddy

Bermuda

I t was the day I buried my sister that I discovered my father
could teleport.

Bobbi, the second daughter, the precious child who could do no
wrong, had died an addict's death, gasping her final breaths into
her squat's dusty carpet. Her stoned companions failed to rouse
in time to help her, if they even tried at all.

At the time, I recalled astonishment that she'd outlived Mom,
who'd squandered what life remained in her chemo-ravaged body
zealously shielding Bobbi from any attempts at intervention.

Mom had succumbed to denial. Nothing and no one could
convince her to stop abetting Bobbi's lifestyle, even as destruc-
tive as it had become.

Dad had doted on Mom with a saint's patience, but she would
still berate him and dismiss his attempts to appease her. Even as
he misplaced his keys and struggled to recall the names of dear
friends, his efforts to be close to her, his beloved wife, seemed to
be in vain.

It hurt me to lose my father to that tumultuous time.

We had gathered at Mom's bedside. The pumps and monitors
had been switched off, and the nurses had removed the tubes and

wires. They'd even brushed her hair, teasing what little was left of it into a semblance of dignity.

Alec and I had married not long before, our union forged just in time for this horrible trial. I remembered how he had cradled my head while whispering soft reassurances.

When the moment Mom finally left us had come and gone, the tears I had expected to release me never arrived. Instead, leaden numbness filled my limbs.

Dad was a picture of strength, though. His soul no longer burdened by angst and melancholy, he seemed even to have grown taller. I was so proud of him at that moment, his cheeks glistening, his eyes reflecting the kind relief that only a cancer death can deliver.

Bobbi stood stoic next to the hospital bed, holding our mother's lifeless hand for nearly ten minutes as she shifted her weight from one foot to the other, humming something. Then, without comment, she left. I didn't expect to see her next as a corpse.

"Dad . . ." I began, after Bobbi's footsteps had echoed away.

He turned to face me and smiled, "Tanya . . ."

My lips began to move, but he placed his finger on my lips.

"Shush," he said to me, deep brown eyes gazing into mine. "It's all okay now. It's all forgiven."

"Forgiven?" I whispered, clutching Alec's arm more tightly.

He nodded wisely and, against reason, I willed myself to believe it.

So it was, years later, at Bobbi's not so well-attended funeral, that I stood alone, dressed in whatever finery I could dust off. My wedding band told a fiction that only I still entertained.

The pastor droned his eulogy to the echoes of that deserted church hall. Bobbi's friends couldn't even pass up one hit just to see her off.

By then, Dad wasn't in any kind of shape to attend. He'd lost much of his ability to separate past and present, and in those months after Alec had finally left for good, I certainly wasn't up to repeatedly explaining to him who had died and when. Or why.

So, he wasn't there to see Bobbi's casket lowered into the ground, or to smell the earthy dampness filling the empty air. Or to weep for that one lost daughter. I did not linger long enough to see them start heaping the dark soil on top of her.

I drove home to darkened windows and an empty driveway. I turned the key and the heavy door to swing ajar, sending white paint chips drifting to the concrete stoop.

Inside, I collapsed onto the couch and immediately fell asleep, exhausted and still wrapped in the dress I'd worn to see my baby sister buried.

It was on that starry, clear night that I awoke to find my father, standing outside, his wiry torso propped nonchalantly against my peeling door frame. Crickets chirped their lonely songs into the dark air. I couldn't tell how late it was.

He was wearing the robe that I'd bought him one Christmas, light-blue flannel pajamas, and ridiculous bunny-eared slippers someone had given him. His skin was yellowed by the bare incandescent bulb dangling from exposed wires.

"What are you doing here, Dad?" I asked drowsily.

"I came to see you, Toots," he answered, rocking a little unsteadily. I had always detested that nickname, but of course, I reasoned, dementia would leave *that* memory intact.

I pulled the dress tighter against the chill breeze and scanned the street behind him, but didn't see the fading taillights of any vehicle that might have left him there.

"How did you get here, Dad?" I asked, shivering a little.

"I just came," he stated plainly.

"Come in, Dad," I sighed, propping the door wide open. "C'mon, it's cold."

I put my arm around his bony shoulders and guided him inside, closing the door behind us. He shuffled his feet a little more than I remembered.

I persuaded him to lie on my worn sofa and then draped a woollen blanket over him, tucking the end up to his chin as he had done for me so many years before.

"'Night, Dad," I murmured as I kissed him goodnight, but he had already fallen asleep. The musty blanket heaved slowly, synchronized with his muted snoring.

I hesitated, staring at his sleeping form before retreating to my bedroom.

"I love you, Daddy," I whispered into the darkness, glad to have him back again.

The following morning, I rose before the sun had fully crested the trees and wandered into the kitchen, passing the empty second bedroom. I sometimes thought about the plans Alec and I had made. Wall colours and boys' names and the right kind of car seat. Two painful losses had doomed our relationship to fights and insults.

"I'm getting breakfast, Dad," I yelled. There'd be enough time to feed us both and return him to the nursing home before work.

There was no response.

"Dad?"

The couch was empty. Just as I began panicking, he emerged, from the tiny bathroom. A foul, dank, earthy smell emerged along with him.

"Dad!" I screamed, rushing past him to slam the door shut. "That really stinks!"

He laughed heartily, a deep chuckle that I wasn't used to hearing, not since I had convinced myself that he couldn't be safe at his own house.

"Would you like to have pancakes?"

"Of course, Bobbi, You always make the best pancakes." He grinned.

"It's Tanya, Dad."

"That's right. Sorry, honey." His broad smile waned. Sometimes, in moments of clarity, he would realize what was happening to him.

"It's okay, Dad."

I didn't bother to remind him that Bobbi had died. Eventually, he would remember on his own and become distraught. It was terrible to observe those moments when the fog lifted just enough to let the demons in.

I made the pancakes while he regaled me with stories about my childhood, as if they had just happened yesterday. He would tell me those same stories four or five times each, but I giggled like a child every time I heard them.

The telephone's ring interrupted the idyll.

After a moment's hesitation, I picked up the handset.

"Mrs. Smith? This is Greg Butler from Cider Oaks Nursing Home . . ." He sounded harried.

"Ms.," I corrected. "I was going to call you . . ."

"Ms. Smith, my apologies. We're required to inform you that we're having difficulty locating your father. He hasn't been checked out and we have no indication that he's even left the facility."

"But, he's here!" I blurted.

"Pardon me?"

"He's with me, at my house. He just showed up last night. We're eating breakfast right now."

A considerable pause elapsed before he spoke again.

"But . . . how did he get there?"

"I don't know," I replied, gazing at the blob of syrup dripping from my father's chin. "He just showed up at my door."

"I . . . ah, right," he said after considerable hesitation. "Well, there's no problem now. We know where he is, so we can call off the search. Go ahead and bring him back whenever you're ready."

"Okay, I'll do that. Thank you, Mr. Butler. I'm really sorry about this."

"I'd like to say it's no trouble, but . . ." he stammered.

"Yes, I appreciate how difficult this must be."

"You have no idea."

"I suppose that's true." I smiled into the mouthpiece. "Thank you, Mr. Butler."

"You're welcome, Ms. Smith. Goodbye."

Before I'd put the handset in its cradle, I heard his voice, yelling faintly.

"Yes? Mr. Butler?"

"Ms. Smith, a request. When you bring him back in, would you have time for a short conversation about this?"

"I think so." I found myself nervously tapping my foot on the floor tiles.

"That would be excellent," he said. "Until then, Ms. Smith."

"Yes. Thanks again, Mr. Butler."

I turned to see my father smiling at me over what remained of the pancakes.

"These are good!" he exclaimed.

Dad graciously suffered the long drive to Cider Oaks, but he became less and less talkative the nearer we got to it. In the end, he just silently watched the passing scenery with the interest of someone who was seeing it all for the first time.

The nurses who greeted us at the cobblestone entrance fawned over my father as if he was some kind of celebrity. He hammed it up, even pinching one of them on the behind. I was mortified, but the nurse looked back and winked at me. It was clear that this was how they managed him.

Only after my father and his entourage had wandered off did I notice a man standing near there.

"Ms. Smith?" He approached me, offering a hand.

"Yes. Mr. Butler is it? It's nice to meet you."

I glanced at my watch.

"I apologise, but I have to be at work in half an hour," I explained.

"That's not a problem." He nodded in sympathy. "This shouldn't take more than five minutes."

He guided me into his office. Folders, binders and loose papers littered the desk's scarred, laminate surface.

"So, this is about my father's ability to leave the nursing home undetected," I began.

"Yes. It's definitely an issue of concern for us," he replied. "And, I must be frank with you, we have no idea how he managed to visit your home last night."

He paused. "There's more to this . . ."

"More?"

"Yes, this isn't the first time your father has . . . relocated."

The way he uttered the word made it clear that it wasn't his first choice.

"What do you mean?" My fingernails were digging shallow 'U' marks into my handbag.

He leaned forward, placing his elbows on the desk. His eyes were wide.

"Ms. Smith. There've been five of these incidents."

"Five!" I shrieked. "Why am I just learning about this now?"

"I'm sorry about that. We weren't trying to deceive you, but so far, we've only considered administrative failures. People have already been terminated over this."

"What explanation could there be?" I began to tremble.

"The first time this happened, your father was asleep in his room when the shift nurse checked. We keep the doors locked for the Alzheimer's patients, because they can wander off and get disoriented."

I nodded. That had been a deciding factor for moving him to the nursing home.

"But the next shift nurse, four hours later, found him hunting around in the recreation room, looking for someone named 'Phillip'."

"The family dog." I smiled.

"Ah, that makes sense." For a moment he seemed to flirt with the idea of asking why someone would name their dog 'Phillip', but decided against it.

He continued. "A week after that, we found him wandering around the cafeteria. He claimed that he was looking for ice cream."

"He does like snacks," I confirmed.

"And then, less than a month ago, he was picked up by one of the security guards while walking along the fence in driving rain. When the guard spoke to him, your father just said something about it being 'time to go home'. Do you have any idea what he might have meant by that?"

I shrugged. "Not really, no."

He leaned back in his chair, which squeaked in protest.

"Unfortunately," he went on, "while we suspect that he's simply managing to take advantage of unlatched doors and gates, our security video isn't of sufficient quality to draw *any* conclusions. We've had a slew of problems with those cameras, despite replacing a bunch."

"And now this," I mumbled, my throat suddenly dry.

I stole a look at my watch and rose from the chair.

"Mr. Butler, I think that we've run out of time." I hadn't heard anything that I wanted to hear.

"Yes, of course, Ms. Smith." He rose, offering his hand. "I trust we can resume this conversation in the near future?"

"Yes, absolutely," I confirmed, accepting the handshake.

As I turned to leave, a question tugging at my conscience made me stop.

"Mr. Butler, are you convinced that my father is still safe here?"

"Certainly. We're devoted to providing the necessary coverage, even if we need to allocate more staff."

His reassurance did nothing to allay my fears.

As I drove away from the complex, I replayed the exchange in my mind, over and over.

I dreamed a telephone was ringing, only to find it to be real. In my sleep, I had clutched the satin pillowcase so desperately that the blood had drained from my fingertips. Perspiration had soaked through my pajamas.

"Hello!" I tried to sound civil.

"Miss Smith?" The voice on the other end sounded distressed.

"Ms. What time is it?"

"Ms. Smith, this is Rebecca at Cider Oaks. Your father is not in his room, or anywhere on the grounds. Is he there with you? I'm so sorry to have to call you like this," she gasped, scarcely taking a breath between sentences.

"No, no. He's not here."

"Ms. Smith, we have no clue as to where he might be. Please let us know if he turns up there."

"Okay, I . . . Wait. Wasn't someone watching him?"

"Oh, oh," she interrupted. "The police are here now, Ms. Smith. I have to talk to them. Can I call you back?"

"Yes, of course," I stammered.

I'd scarcely had the time to start imagining all the terrible outcomes when the phone rang again.

"Rebecca, did you find . . . ?" I began.

"Tanya! Tanya, is that you?" The caller was shouting.

"Yes. YES!" I yelled. "Who is this?"

"Tanya! This is Deborah Tang. Do you remember me?"

Recognition was gradual, but the woman's voice was tied to many of my childhood memories.

"Mrs. Tang!" I said at last. "Yes, of course I remember you. How are you?"

I recalled the woman's living room and her daughters, Mindy and Anh–and the smell of freshly baked chocolate chip cookies on Sunday afternoons.

"Tanya, your father is at the house! Did you know? He's trying to get inside, but it's all boarded up. He's trying to get in but I don't want him to get hurt!"

I tried not to dwell on how my father had managed to travel more than a hundred kilometres from the nursing home to the place where we'd once been a family. I had been heartbroken when I signed the contract for the house to become someone else's. In the end, though, the family who bought it also failed to hang onto it.

"I'm telling the police now, Mrs. Tang," I said. "They're going to come and help him, okay?"

"Tell them not to hurt him," she insisted. "He's so nice. Tell them to be careful."

"I will, Mrs. Tang. Thank you so much!"

"Bobbi! I'm okay! There's nothing wrong with me," my father insisted. His eyes wandered around the room.

I stood outside the holding cell. They'd put him in it "for his safety", they said, but I could still barely contain my rage as I watched them unlock the barred door.

I waited patiently as police officers released him.

"It's alright now, Dad. We're just going to get you back to the nursing home, okay?"

"I just want to go home, Bobbi," he said, hurt and fear in his face.

"I know, Daddy," I said. "It's okay."

I felt heartbroken again, as I helped his once strong body climb into the passenger seat of my car.

We drove in silence while he slowly calmed down. I was relieved when at last he fell asleep, snoring rhythmically, though the long journey to Cider Oaks was lonely without a conversation to fill the air, even recycled stories from the past.

I drove on, but when I turned to look at his sleeping form, he vanished without a whisper. I didn't register his disappearance at first. I could see the passenger seat where his tall frame should have been and the night view beyond the window pane was starkly unobscured. Red and white vehicle lights danced in the glass.

I screamed so much that I couldn't continue driving. The tires screeched in protest, and only grace allowed me to stop the car without crashing into something. My fingertips uselessly clutched the steering wheel, without sensation. The engine's idling rumble filled a nighttime stillness, only broken occasionally by the wail of far-off truck tires.

I stared at the vacant passenger seat, willing it to magically yield back my father.

After some time, I gathered my senses enough to resume driving back to the house that Alec had deserted. I pondered who to call, who would believe me.

I'd barely crossed the threshold when I saw the answering machine's blinking red light.

Hesitantly, I pressed the winking button.

"Mrs. Smith . . ." began the first message, "this is Sergeant Yates at Brookline police station. Your father appears to have returned to your old family home . . ."

I skipped the message, unable to bear listening to it.

"Tanya! This is Deborah Tang . . ."

Again I pressed the skip button.

"Ms. Smith, Greg Butler here. Your father appeared here briefly . . ."

Sobbing, I pressed the skip button once more.

"Toots . . ."

I froze, my finger suspended motionless.

"Daddy? Daddy? Is that you?"

"I stopped by the house," his voice continued, "but Bobbi and your mom aren't there . . ."

"I know, Dad," I bleated. "Bobbi and Mom are dead. Phillip's dead . . ."

"So I'm going to go and find them. It won't take long, though, so don't worry."

It had been years since I heard my father speak with authority like that. He sounded like the father who'd carried me on his shoulders, whose knee I'd bounced on. The first man to tell me I was beautiful.

"No, Dad. Come here to me," I pleaded. "They've all gone, it's just us now. Stay with me, Daddy, I need you!"

". . . I love you, baby. I'll be back soon. Be good, okay?"

"Daddy, don't go," I bawled, but the message had ended.

Months later, there still was no sign of him. There were no more calls or messages. No sightings.

Cider Oaks ended their involvement after the police investigation eliminated any culpability on their part. I could only imagine how ecstatic they'd become once their liability ended.

Evidently, the answering machine's recording was the only thing that stood between me and a murder charge. I guffawed when a detective admitted that to me, the sudden outburst provoking a look normally reserved for the certifiably insane.

I didn't get fired, though. Miraculously. Though I spent my working days mindlessly processing reams of unremarkable paperwork, I was, to my amazement, still able to get the job done correctly.

Months passed, but the hole in my heart didn't seem to diminish much, though I hadn't expected it would.

Then one mild Saturday afternoon, as I was vacantly watching reruns of some once popular comedy, lying on the couch, wrapped to the neck in a ratty blanket, a voice in my head suddenly wondered if there was any mail in the roadside mailbox.

Just as suddenly, I found myself standing at the curb, next to that very mailbox, with the blanket still draped around me. The TV remote control dangled loosely from my fingertips. Condensed breath puffed from my nostrils into the cool air. A runner took note of my still blanketed attire, but that was the only attention I seemed to have attracted.

I opened the creaky mailbox lid and extracted the two or three envelopes that had collected there. Slowly, as the shock abated, a calm understanding remained in its place.

For the first time in years I began to beam, grinning broadly enough to make the muscles in my cheeks cramp.

Above the quiet rustling of autumn leaves, I whispered, "It's okay, Daddy, I'll just come to *you.*"

BRIAN FRANKLIN

Quaka-Hadja

Barbados

L ia stared into the mirror, plucking at her Kanekalon eyebrows beneath a pale light. Her body jerked with each movement of her arms. Although well-made, the tweezers wouldn't work: never fully depressing when she squeezed (try as best as she could), and slipping from her fingers to poke one eye or the other. She screwed up her face and tried again. This time she managed to grab a hair before the tweezers shot from her hand and skittered beneath the sink.

Sighing, she felt about for the tweezers on creaking knees, finding them just as she was about to give up.

She took up the magazine again to compare her work with the glossy image of the pouting woman with the thin, high eyebrows. She fought back another sigh. What more she could do? Perhaps she'd be better off plucking out all the hairs and painting two lines in their place.

The little clock on the wall chirped. *Oh nine hundred already?* She pressed off the alarm, wondering where the night had gone. With one last look at the mirror she tucked the tweezers behind her left ear and turned to leave.

The light flashed, then the room went dark. She wrapped her hands about herself, shivering until it came back on. *Yuh t'ink something wrong with the turbine? Maybe the wires get fray?*

She headed for the study.

Dust lingered in the bars of light leaking through the shuttered windows. Before the furthest bookcase a man sat in a wide leather chair, his feet propped on a pouffe. She brushed the chair's peeling skin from his shoulders. "So, wha' yuh t'ink?" she asked. She nudged him, smiled at him, but he didn't reply. Father said little these days.

He seemed to return her smile, though, and she grinned. "I did reading the magz like yuh say. Mum's in there, yuh did know dah?" She took one from the stack on the coffee table nearby, flipped through the pages until she came upon the coquettish gaze of a dark woman who looked *almost* like her. She held it up to him. "Look, she right here so! I gine be real pretty like she jes' now, and then we can go watch them moobies yuh always talking 'bout with all yuh friends."

She rested the magazine back on the stack, stepped closer to the old man. For a little while she plucked grey hairs from his beard—the tweezers always worked better on him—and brushed dust from his haggard face. She put down the tweezers and held his left hand in both of hers.

"Yuh hungry? I gine mek we breakfast. I know it ain't never nuh good, but I getting better, see? I coming back jes' now."

The *tap-tap* of her footsteps on the kitchen tiles seemed louder than ever. Lia flicked the light switch but the room remained in shadow. *Oh no! It mash up!* She rubbed the knots in her arms, over and over. The motion calmed her. She glanced up at the fluorescent lights sunk in the paint-bubbled ceiling. They had been flickering of late but she had changed them and they seemed fine. *Wha' wrong with them now? I gotta try and fix them lata.*

She hurried to the windows to open the curtains.

Through the frosted glass she could make out little besides

the impressions of shapes, hear nothing but the wind sough-
ing past the cracks in the pane. Once, she had believed a whole
city stood out there. Glimmering buildings like those of Paris or
New York.

"No, Lia," Father's voice came back to her. "Jes' sand and ash.
And memory."

Behind her, the shadows had softened, curling away from the
light. She went to the cupboard and threw open the doors. Nibbled her thumbs as she considered its contents.

Tins of meat, bottles of oil, boxes of tea, biscuits, rice. She
would have to restock soon, but this should be enough for a little
while, wouldn't it? Father had never told her where he shopped.

Lia reached for a can of corned beef with her left hand but
found that her fingers were stiff, clumsy, her elbow grinding and
popping. Using her right instead, she took out the can, a bottle
of honey and a pack of crackers and rested them on the counter.

She pried off the tin's top with a tin-opener she found in the
drawer, sniffed the meat. It smelled like nothing. She ripped open
the pack of biscuits with a knife and spread the meat between
two wafers. The meat's texture was as tough as she was used to,
so it was still good, right? She drizzled honey about it. A bit of
sweetness he wouldn't expect! She smiled and for a moment her
eyes drifted towards the stove.

She had never used it.

"Keep from oil and fire, you hear me!" Father had said on
more than one occasion, sometimes as he stood by the kitchen
window staring into his past reflected in its frost, or hunched
over her creaking legs in the workshop.

"Why?" she would ask.

"You's jes' a quaka-hadja," he would say. Half in a whisper,
almost to himself. "Jes' a lil puppet. Wood and old bone and plastic and steel. Ain't really complete neither. A.I. need wuk. Cahn
smell, taste . . . not yet." He would sigh. "Still half a woman."

She would stare at him, blinking plastic eyelids under the white light. A question would form on her lips, but seeing it and running his fingers along the knots in her arms he would reply, "Jes' do as I say, hear?"

But the magazines said that fire made food better. The images of fried meats and fish flashed across her mind's eye but she blinked them away, turned back to making her corned beef sandwich. For lunch she would do something really special. She picked up a bit of the meat on her finger, eased it into her mouth. It tasted like cardboard, but didn't everything?

When she had plated the meal as nicely as she could, she placed it on a tray and headed back to the study. The sun rose towards midday in the world beyond the shutters. Yes, she was a little late and that was happening more and more often, but Father wouldn't mind. His eyes, barely open, seemed to follow her movements. Shadows deepened the creases on his forehead.

"Here you go!" Lia said.

He remained still.

"Um . . . doan smell so good, nuh?" She frowned and held the plate up to her nose but again smelled nothing. "You ain't gine give it a try?"

He had one hand over his chest, gripping his cotton shirt, the other splayed across the chair handle, almost touching one of half a dozen glasses of water on the table close by. The sparkle of his eyes dimmed in the shadow between the steadily shifting bars of light.

Lia moved to shake him but hesitated. "He fall 'sleep," she told herself in a whisper. "He does sleep fuh so long these days."

"I'll rest this here fuh when yuh wake up, a'ight?" she said to him, resting the tray on his lap. "I gine down to the workshop now. I need to fix the lights in the kitchen. I also gotta find some grease for these joints—yuh did hear them, right?" She moved her squeaking arm. "Please doan worry, I ain't gine be very long."

Outside the door, she waited a bit to see if he would take a bite when he thought she wasn't looking. He didn't move. Maybe he could still see her from the corner of his eye and was smiling to himself, slowly shaking his head. He'd always been fond of her little games.

Down the wooden steps that creaked as loudly as her knees, Lia pushed through the stone door into the workshop. A single bulb hung on a wire from the roof, its light bleaching the up-turned tables and chairs and the slab of concrete upon which she had been birthed. Against the far wall was a mirror nearly the wall's width and as high as the roof. The floors and walls were featureless save for the wriggling crack in one corner. About the crack were the green-brown stains of algae and moss. Moisture glistened like eyes.

She hurried to the crack, rested a piece of the corned-beef-on-biscuit by it. She sat on the ground and watched until a centipede peered out, tasting at the air with its huge feelers. Slipping out towards the biscuit, he (she assumed it was a he) caught it, forced the meat into his hidden mouth with his pincers. He moved slower than usual. He was so skittish, usually. Maybe he was finally growing to like her, to feel more at ease when she was around. She'd watched him grow from a small, threadlike thing to now about eight inches long and just under an inch wide. All large reddish-brown segments and golden, pointed legs. Over the minutes and hours and days the moss around his hole had become thicker, joined by tiny brown mushrooms and thin-leafed plants like black hairs.

"How you?" Lia asked.

The centipede twitched from the meat, seeming to glance at her, trying to taste her scent on the air.

"You'd eat anything I cook, nuh?"

He lifted his head off the ground for a moment. Twisted it to the left and the right. Turned and slipped back into the dankness inside the wall.

She went to the tools laid in rows beside the slab. Light glinted off their polished surfaces—as well they should since she cleaned them every day at 0600 hours. The oil can was on a nearby shelf. She poured a few drops onto each finger joint on her left hand, then on her elbows and knees. She pivoted each joint until the squeaks faded. She replaced the can, saw that there wasn't very much left. It probably wouldn't last the week.

With a screwdriver, Lia tightened the bolts in her legs and arms. Used the cheesecloth to buff her breasts and stomach. She felt less depressed when she finished, even if she still probably didn't look too much like the girls in the magazines. She checked the clock. Two hours later. God! That was thirty minutes more than she should have taken but . . . who cared? Who *cared?* Father cared, right? He meant her to operate on a fixed schedule. She had to account for each second. *But who cared, nuh?* She wondered at the strange thought.

From a shelf at the back of the workshop, she took a fresh fluorescent bulb.

Back upstairs, Father's meal lay undisturbed. Only a film of dust and sand now covered the plate. His hands were in the same positions. Mouth still drawn into a loose grimace, lips slightly open as if to speak. His head angled back, nostrils wide.

"Um did really bad, nuh? I sorry. I gine do something different now."

She took the tray and hurried to the kitchen. He shouldn't have missed breakfast like that and it was all her fault. It wasn't healthy to miss the first meal of the day, especially since it'd been so late. She'd have to cook something bigger, more filling, tastier. Something he couldn't resist.

As she changed the bulb in the kitchen, her mind raced: *He tell muh he love flying-fish, but never let muh cook it. Chicken too. Lamb. Cou-cou and steam' veg and sea-egg. But he say there ain't nuh more sheep, nuh more chicken, nuh fish. Nuh nothing.*

The light outside the window seemed darker under the flare of the new bulb. Thunder rumbled through the roof. Cups and bowls clinked together behind the cupboards' glass panes.

She placed a pot and frying pan on the stove, opened a small bag of rice, a can of beans and Spam from a drawer. In there she had stashed a cooking magazine, folded open to a recipe she had always imagined preparing. It looked easy:

INGREDIENTS
2 cups water
1 cup long grain rice
1 ½ cup kidney beans
1 container Spam
1 tbsp sunflower oil

DIRECTIONS
Bring water to a boil in a pot, then add rice. When fluffy, remove from flame.
Add oil in a frying pan. Heat until hot but not smoking.
Add beans to frying pan. Wait 5 minutes then add the Spam. Stir. Allow to cook for 10 more minutes.

Her freshly oiled hands moved quickly, noiselessly. But as she turned to get the matches out of the cupboard she hesitated. She'd be disobeying Father. Something resisted the notion, made it feel wrong. Her joints felt rusted in the new oil. Her eyes widened, each breath a wheeze, each moment a closing vice about her limbs.

She needed to stop. To turn away from the cupboard. Away from the stove. Back to the simple, easy meals Father didn't seem to like anymore.

No, no! I gine through with this!

Lia pushed against the stiffness, forced her hands to move to the cupboard.

"He need to eat!" she said through gritted teeth. "Three meals a day. Lots of water. Keep him looking decent. Talk and talk and talk to him, in the dialect of his old Barbadian homeland. Keep the place clean. Look like the girls in his magazines. These are the things he needs."

She had the matches before she realised that she'd overcome the resistance. Quickly now, before it returned! She grabbed the little piece of wood, her hands sweaty with oil. She struck it. Watched it spark then die. Another one. Another. Finally a little flame, steady as a thin knife's blade.

She opened the gas for the burner below the pot of water. Heard it hiss but smelled nothing—had all of that gone too?—held the match near.

Fire ignited about her fingers.

Lia rushed to the sink as the fire engulfed both her arms, fed on her sweat. She spun the faucet open. It coughed, trembled before spitting a stream of bilgy water that slowly cleared. She thrust both hands into it. Cupped water up onto her arms. Sparks and grey smoke filled the sink, swirled past her eyes.

When the fire was out she closed the faucet. She stared at her burnt arms, so dark. Her fingernails melted and scuffed. *Oh God! Oh GodohGodohGod!* Father would know she'd disobeyed. He'd be angry. But what choice did she have? He was hungry! She looked back to the food. That would have to be her apology.

On the stove, fire licked the pot's bottom. She poured in the rice but couldn't bring herself to light the other burner. So she waited until the rice swelled, white and puffy, before lifting the pot off and sliding the frying pan into its place. The oil sizzled as she emptied the beans and Spam into the pan. She thought it should smell great, but there was nothing.

She turned off the gas and watched the flame die. She laid out the food on a big plate, just like in the cooking magazine. Her rice was browner, the Spam a bit darker, but overall a good job.

She put the big plate on a tray with a knife and fork. Pulling on some gloves to hide her burns, she then hurried to the study.

"Look! Look! I get through. Nice and hot too! Come, tek um before um get cold." She held the tray out to Father. "Wha' you waiting fuh?"

Her hands tightened around the tray's edges, her teeth grinding against each other with a slow, metallic, filing sound.

"I put um together real nice. I use the fire . . . um . . . um didn't so bad. And um smell real good, so wha' wrong wid um? Tell me, nuh?"

Silence.

"Tell muh! Yuh . . . yuh fucking, rassgate poppit!"

That was a phrase that should have made him angry, but there was no reaction.

Was this the silent treatment they wrote about in the relationship magazines? But how could she have made him so angry that he wouldn't eat anything she brought him? *I ain't do all he want me to do?*

Oily tears greased her cheeks, dripping onto the tray, oozing over the cutlery. She blinked them away. She needed to look prettier, that was all. Her arms were really too fat. The dark knots in her brown skin unsightly. He'd always said so. None of the women in the magazines had these things. No steel joints punctured their unblemished flesh. Once, he had tried to fix all that, but had lost interest and gone still. Like a stopped clock.

So be it then.

Lia ate the food in the workshop. She tried luring the centipede back out, but he wouldn't come. She left a few forkfuls of the Spam by his hole.

After, she studied her imperfections in the mirror. And with a magazine beside her, opened to a two-page spread of a naked woman with chocolate skin, she set to work.

* * *

She shaved her arms and legs with the plane, counting each strip of wood-flesh as it curled to the floor. She stopped when they were as thin as she could get without cutting into her circuit veins. Paint now, to cover up the joints, and a dark varnish to hide the knots and rings, making her complexion more radiant. Her breasts she rounded more, tapered them to the nipples, for added perkiness. Her hair was curly; the ones in the magazine were straight, but she had no idea how to get it like that.

She turned in the mirror, smiling and raising her hands above her head like the ballerina on Page 57.

Almost there. Almost.

Now for the details. What first—freckles? She applied these with the thin nose of a soldering iron pressed quickly and gently against her hands, feet and face. Now what about . . . ? As she turned, she saw the centipede outside his hole, lying beside the food she'd left for him.

"I know yuh did hear muh," she said, kneeling before him.

He lay on his back, feelers stiff, each leg spasming. Lia bent over him. She'd never seen him do this before.

"Yuh know, Father done talk to muh. I ain't sure wha' I do he." She crossed her arms and pouted for emphasis, but the centipede didn't seem to notice.

"Yuh ignoring muh too?" She poked it and it jerked away, flicking its tail at her, barely missing. "Boy! You near scratch me, yuh! Wha' I do you now?"

The centipede's twisting slowed, his body curling into a red-and-black half-circle.

Lia ran a finger along his back, but he didn't jerk away this time. Maybe that's how he liked it—a smooth touch, not a poke in the belly.

"Well, sorry. Yuh could'a say somet'ing. Look, try and eat wha' I leff yuh. Seem like you's the only body dah does appreciate muh food."

The workshop's light blinked and went off. The darkness stretched for longer than before. Lia nibbled her thumbs as she waited for it to come back on. She had to check the wires. She'd been putting that off for far too long. Picking up the toolbox, a lamp and a roll of copper wire from the top shelf, she walked toward the workshop door.

"I coming back jes' now," she said to the centipede.

Outside the workshop, she pushed open the door opposite it. There was another stairway, leading steeply down below flickering bulbs. She made sure to close the door and wait for the hiss of air from its sides and the quiet droning beep that indicated it had sealed properly. She switched on the lamp when the bulbs failed to come back on. Beneath its red blaze she came to another door, circular, with a small oval panel in its face. To her right was a table covered with backpacks of every size, on her left a rack of weathered beige suits. Father had worn these when he went outside (to shop and for some fresh air, he used to say), but they were much too bulky for her. Most had been damaged. Tears and scuffs in the nylon. Broken faceplates, half-melted air tubes. But she'd fixed them. Found all the parts in the workshop on that night when Father had stumbled through the door, his suit burned, boots eaten-away. Her name upon his ragged lips. Lia blinked away the memory of him lying on the floor, scratching at his skin through the holes in the suit's arms.

She shrugged into a suit. Zipped it up, fitted the helmet. Stuffed the roll of wire and toolbox into a backpack she slipped over both shoulders. She went to the panel.

"Hey, Door."

"Lia," the Door droned. "Power failure imminent. Emergency stores critical. Multiple breaches detected. Atmospheric–"

"I know dah! You always sayin' the same t'ing. You ain't even ask me how I doing."

A pause. Static. "Are you having a good day, Lia?"

"Nah. Not like yuh care, though. Open fuh me, please."

The door shuddered. With a terrible groan it rolled two feet to her right then stopped.

"Yuh couldn't ease some more out the way? Is a good t'ing I small," she said, squeezing out into a narrow tunnel.

Along the wall to her right ran a thick wire—the house's power cable. She followed its length, making sure there wasn't any damage to it, until it vanished behind a sheet of paling that used to seal the tunnel's mouth. Now it slammed against the walls, opening and being thrown quickly back. The world beyond it seemed bright enough, so she left the lamp on the ground.

Lia went to the paling. Rough iron and exposed nails were scoring tracks in the concrete with each gust of wind. She'd have to time her move exactly. Moving as closely as she dared, she counted the seconds between the slams. Three. Four. Two. Three point five. The paling opened and she flung herself through. Slipping past just as it was hurled back against the wall. Nails scraping her faceplate.

She ran her fingers about it and her suit frantically, looking for damage. Apart from the scratch across her vision, everything else seemed fine. She sighed, looked out across the landscape through the orange light of late evening sinking into nighttime murk.

Wind-blasted sand raked her suit as the sky barked thunder. Nothing up there but churning red clouds and pink sheet lightning. Against the sky, buildings caved like melted candles. Blackened spires. Concrete-iron ribs open to the elements. Gutted.

Checking every inch of the wire, she moved slowly until she saw the wind turbine. Its head turned in the gale but its blades—made of lashed-together corrugated iron, plastic and steel—weren't moving. A sudden fear held her rusted to the ground. *Um . . . like um gone bad or somet'ing?* She couldn't tell. She'd never climbed it—Father did that. But he had shown her his wind turbine magazine once, the one with the white paper pages and pencil diagrams and his name in the bottom left-hand corner of the covers.

She made for it, up a hill sprinkled with the bones of hands and feet and skulls worn almost to shapeless forms in the sand. Quaka-hadja material, Father had called them once. Sisters and brothers waiting to be set to a new schedule. They snapped and forced her feet from under her many times. She got up, each step slower than the last, raising her hand above her forehead to fend off the worst of the sand so she could see.

At its base, finally. The wind turbine shivered and groaned, pulled against its supports buried deep beneath the ground of collapsed superstructures. Its head vanished for a moment within a cloud of sand and ash. Remembering the map from Father's magazine, Lia found and pulled a lever nearby to lock the blades in place so they wouldn't cut her arms off when she got the turbine working.

She started up the rungs set into the wind turbine's sides. All seemed quiet. Just the thunder and her breath hissing through set teeth. Wind curled around her arms and back, tugging her so, as if to say, "Let go, nuh?" Looking down, she could no longer see the ground. But around her lightning lanced the air and flicked from one concrete-iron rib to the next.

Lia huddled against the rungs. Eyes closed. "I gotta do um!" she told herself. "I gotta do um. Cahn let he live in the dark." Opening her eyes she glanced up. She was almost there.

At the top of the rungs the wind turbine's head appeared vast and alone. She moved towards its back and found that sand had built up in the motor controls, jamming the blades. Some of the wires were exposed, their casings sheared off.

She crouched and took out her toolbox. Pulled Father's diagrams into her mind's eye. Scrolled through them until one matched the motor controls. Following the annotations, she cleared the machinery as best she could, duct-taped the exposed wires. Greased what joints she could get at with the oil as the wind grew stronger. Between it and her naked circuitry nothing but re-stitched fabric.

"Dah's it," she whispered to herself. "Leh we see if um gine work."

She crawled back down. Step after step. Stopping when the terror of the ravaging wind and shaking turbine grew too much, starting when she pushed through the fear. At the bottom, she hurried to the lever and pulled it.

The blades up above spun. In fits at first. Then going so fast she couldn't make them out.

"See?" She said to her doubt. She smiled, rested her hands on her small hips. "I get um wukking again! I do everyt'ing he want."

Something in her wanted to stay here. Perhaps head down the other side of the hill towards the shattered buildings half hidden in debris and sand. There were only so many pretty places in the magazine. Perhaps there were more behind the horizon of dust and ash and wind-eaten ruins that fenced this world in. It wasn't like Father would miss her.

But no.

She would continue cooking, fixing, cleaning, looking pretty. He couldn't stay silent forever.

Past Imperfect

Trinidad & Tobago

She stared at the withered, mousy-looking husk of a man who stood outside the door to her new office. A pathetic, crooked shell of a human being, buried in layers of rags that looked too heavy for his frail frame. Even amongst the stubborn dregs of humanity, he seemed a hopeless case. If he was here looking for help she could offer no miracles.

Then recognition dawned. She knew who her visitor must be. So this was the man who remembered everything. She honestly did not know what she had expected, but this was disheartening.

"You're the record keeper?" she asked. "The one with the photographic memory?"

He nodded.

"What's that like . . . ? Your earliest memories, how vivid are they?"

"Picture a face," he told her. "One that you know well; one never far from your mind. A face that makes you feel at home, that makes you happy and, perhaps, at the same time sad. A distant face, distorted by years of longing and regret. Picture that face warm and smiling, a reminder of a life worth living. Imagine watching it shatter like porcelain, explode into a dozen pieces that . . ."

He stopped. Cloudy eyes that had been staring through her

seemed to refocus. "Sorry Doc," he said, eyes suddenly fixed on the ground. "But how the hell was I *supposed* to respond?"

She stared at him for several seconds. "You look like shit," she declared.

"And a pleasure to meet you too." He gave a tip of the hat, tugging on the edge of his black, woollen cap. "Just to get it outta the way, have you any other prying questions to ask?"

"None for now. Little afraid of what you'd say next."

A smiling, youthful visage briefly filled her thoughts, and she braced the barriers in her mind—dams that held back the torrent of bitter memories. If she let them crack now, the flood might overwhelm her.

"Can't be thin-skinned. Not if you've lasted *this* long . . . Thought myself unflappable by now. It was . . . *interesting* to be proven wrong."

"I try," the decrepit man said with a sheepish grin, flashing a few rotten teeth and blackened gums.

"Why?"

He stared at her blankly. It was unsettling, but then he looked away, as if embarrassed.

"No, really," she insisted, observing the odd little tics in his face. "Why?"

He shrugged weakly, an almost imperceptible movement. Even so, she got the impression that the effort caused him pain. The change in his expression was even more fleeting than the shrug. He hid it with a practised swiftness.

"It's my job, I suppose," he said. "At least it is now. It was different in the beginning. Still remember details of purifying water with ozone, generated by electrolysis or electrical arcing apparatus. Just don't ask me to build the damn things. *That* was never my job. And now . . . . Now I'm supposed to help people *feel*, remember. Or help them pretend . . . Pretend they're someone else, someone not here. For whatever that's worth."

He waved dismissively with his right hand, which he then flexed slowly.

"Not in love with your job?" she asked, while eyeing the uneven way that his gloved fingers moved.

"Doc," he said, shaking his head. "Maybe doctorin' is what you've always wanted to do since before the world went to shit. Great for you. But some of us just have roles. I do my part, and I get a chunk of petrified bread or a semi-edible rock every few days, and a little water that someone else made safe to drink."

His eyes darted from side to side as he spoke. She was reminded of a patient she had treated in another life. An autistic child with a broken wrist and a fretful, hovering mother. The entire time, the girl's eyes had wandered like that.

There had been a few others she knew who were on the spectrum. None had so closely matched that girl's behaviour. Human connection had seemed much harder for the child to deal with than the pain of her injury. Perhaps this man was the same.

How many years had it been since she had seen that girl—since she had seen any child?

"Help people pretend, huh? Difficult in a world as poisoned and barren as this. Providing escape from reality sounds like quite a rewarding job, role, or whatever you want to call it."

The man's roving eyes suddenly snapped to hers. He cocked his head to the side, seeming to focus on something at the back of her skull, seeming to listen to something in the distance, audible only to him.

"It's not *my* escape," he said.

She did not know what to make of him. She doubted that his capabilities matched what had been described. She doubted that he could touch his own toes. But he definitely piqued her interest.

"You're a curiosity," she said. "Guess it's a welcome change from the monotony slowly killing us all. But goddamn, you really do look like shit."

"You know what? You caught me on a bad day. I forgot to comb my hair this morning."

"I'm pretty sure you're bald under there."

"Huh? When did that happen?" He pushed his gloved fingers beneath his cap, raising it enough to reveal that the only thing underneath was more pale, wrinkled skin.

"Then I guess you caught me on a bad decade." His smile was far from warm or comforting.

It was odd. He presented as socially challenged and introverted, but could also seem remarkably personable. This was her most involved conversation in years. His ghoulish appearance and attempts at humour were unsettling, but he also observed social niceties that had long since atrophied from most interactions.

She looked past him to the armed guard standing in front of another metal door, further down the narrow hallway. He stared impassively at the grimy wall opposite him and barely even glanced in their direction.

"Not to be too blunt, Doc . . ."

She looked back at her visitor.

"I'm playing my role, and you're getting something outta that. Something that might be important to you."

He held up his gloved hands, contorted into claws. He looked at them with an expression of resignation.

"But it won't be long before it ends. My hands will go, and then I'll starve." His tone was matter-of-fact. "So, can you help me, Doc?"

"You know, when your people told me about you, they neglected to mention that you were a crumbling human wreck with busted hands."

Of course they hadn't. They'd wanted her to come with them willingly, after all.

"That your professional diagnosis?"

She gave him another once-over with her eyes.

"Probably not far off."

He was right. There were no jobs anymore, no careers, no professions. There was just finding a place; doing whatever got you to tomorrow.

"Tell you what . . . In the interest of professionalism, I'll do a proper examination, and *then* make a determination. Maybe you're not nearly in as bad a state as you look. Come in."

She stepped aside and pulled the door fully open for him, watching as he surveyed the room with eyes that were more active than before. His gaze settled on the large metal desk that was its centrepiece. Boxes were stacked on one side of it, packed with books, papers, ancient and patched-together medical instruments, and other odds and ends—all relics of her previous home.

She had lived in a small camp with few able hands, maybe two working guns, and even less ammunition. When strangers arrived with automatic rifles and stern expressions, they had faced no resistance. They had marched her out of the makeshift tent that had doubled as office and operating theatre, grabbing anything that looked useful on the way.

It was funny in a sick sort of way. Her old group had only recently settled in this area, fleeing violent scavengers. The scavengers had known to stay clear. They had known that this place was home to a large and well-equipped colony, one that could take whatever—or whomever—it wanted from anyone in its territory.

However, her abductors *had* promised recompense of sorts for her services as a physician. Recompense, but no choice. Not really. Now here she was in this rundown concrete fortress at the centre of the settlement with the man who was supposed to make good on those promises.

They had put her in a building that had once been a community centre, but now bore the marks of several violent confrontations. Like the large hole in the wall which let the early morning gloom into her second-storey office. The man's eyes lingered there as well, tracing the jagged edges of shattered stonework, then studying the rickety set of shelves on the wall that now held a few faded, old medical tomes.

She closed the door behind him and hobbled over to the desk, wincing at the familiar pain in her hip. Carefully lowering herself into her chair, she motioned him to the one opposite. The two chairs and the desk were the only pieces of furniture that her new hosts had provided–two more pieces than she'd had in her old tent. Even with her fading sense of hearing, her visitor's joints creaked audibly as he folded himself into the chair.

"So what ails you, *specifically?*" she asked.

There was little point to the question. But she supposed that it was procedure. At least it had been, once upon a time.

"Well, Doc," he sighed, holding his hands up in front of him. "As I said, my hands are in pretty bad shape. Loss of dexterity, hard to move my fingers, the joints click and grind; lots of pain."

"A problem given your work, I imagine."

"It's not ideal."

He smiled wryly.

"Remove the gloves. Let me take a look."

"It's been a long time since I last saw these naked," he said, flexing gloved fingers. "Easier to write with the gloves on than to let the cold touch them."

He struggled to remove the woollen coverings. She rose unsteadily and moved to his side of the desk, leaning over to examine his mangled hands. It was not a pretty sight. His joints were severely inflamed. There were several nodules on and around them, each over a centimetre wide and firm to the touch. Some of his fingers bent in unnatural ways.

"Have difficulty getting up in the morning?" she asked, as she traced her fingers along his deformed joints.

"Got my own place," he replied, wincing as she bent one of his less mutilated digits. "Got a cot in the basement of a quaint little hovel a few blocks from here. What's left of it. It's mostly rubble now, really. Anyway, it gets cold down there. So I'm always really stiff and weak in the morning. Getting up the stairs is a real bitch. But, at least, I'm usually warmed up enough by the time I limp over here that the pain is easier to manage."

She suspected that the early morning fatigue and stiffness had little to do with the temperature of his dwelling place. They were common symptoms of certain types of arthritis.

"Why live out there?" she asked, pressing her hand against his forehead. He recoiled from the unexpected contact.

High temperature. She had expected as much.

"Do you find that you're often feverish?"

"Comes and goes. When it hits me in the morning it's almost impossible to get out of bed."

"So again, why so far? It's a difficult trek over here. It's probably dangerous to have no one around. Don't most of your people sleep in the rooms downstairs?"

She had seen many cots in one of the large meeting rooms on the ground floor. A few had still been occupied.

"I . . . like the quiet."

It was hard for her to imagine that this place ever got particularly noisy. There were not that many people around, even compared to her old home, and people were quieter now, in general. Like that guard in the hallway. Resigned. No intensity or bluster.

"You know," he said, almost wistfully, "it used to be different. There used to be a lot more of us out there, in the town. It was safer in here, sure, but there were too many to fit in the building . . . Too many to sustain . . . We're sitting in a tomb." The wistfulness was gone. "Dead men, women and children in the hallways, on the stairs, on their makeshift beds; starved, frozen, or just simply expired. And yet *here* we are . . . chatting on their grave."

His voice was flat and low, almost a whisper.

"Do you remember them?" she asked quietly, as she hobbled back to her seat.

He had not inquired about her diagnosis yet. She imagined that there was little that she could tell him that he did not already suspect. Including how little she could do to help.

"Do you remember the faces of everyone who died here?"

"Of course," he said with a dry chuckle. "It's what I do, right? It's my role, my *gift.*"

Now he was beginning to look agitated.

"To me the corpses are fresh; the blood stains not yet faded to grey—not everyone died of exposure, thirst, or hunger. I still see the spot out there where some kid got his skull caved in, probably because someone else thought he was hoarding crackers. See him every time I walk down that hall, along with the half dozen other corpses in the pile with him."

He glanced at the closed door before continuing.

"But I've never been in here before. Can't see whatever horrors once filled *this* space."

She recalled the way that he had scanned the room when he first entered.

"I'd still like you to describe how your memory works," she told him. "Preferably, without talk of exploding heads."

He stared at her intently for several seconds.

"You got any good news for me, Doc?" he finally asked, looking down at the mangled claws that were his hands.

"*Honestly?*"

"Spent a long time facilitating fantasy and self-delusion. I find that those things have lost most sense of value for me."

"Then, no," she told him, flatly. "You have arthritis. Physical indicators coupled with fever suggests rheumatoid. Could be psoriatic. It's hard to see lesions with so little light on such mottled skin, and the fever could be caused by an unrelated infection. Those are certainly common enough these days.

"Either way, I can't help. Don't even have ibuprofen for your inflammation, which is the most severe case that I've ever seen. Your hands will probably be unusable very soon. I'm surprised that they aren't already. I'm guessing that you weren't expecting better news."

He shrugged weakly.

"Like I said, Doc, not really into self-delusion."

He glanced at the hole in the wall once more.

"So . . ." he breathed out heavily, putting immense weight into the tiny word, "you want me to explain myself to you; how my mind works. And I assume that you still want me to use my *gift* for your benefit, while I still can. But there's nothing you can do for me. Gotta say, this seems like a dismayingly one-way relationship."

"Feeling unmotivated?"

He nodded. "Yeah. Nothing personal."

The man looked smaller than ever, as if his fragile frame was about to crumple and collapse in on itself.

"Look," he said, forlornly. "I know that there's a fast approaching expiration date on me. I bring one thing to the table that keeps me fed. And as soon as my hands go, or my eyes go, or my . . . I start going senile tomorrow, my rations would disappear and I'd starve. You can't actually help me. So I might as well just get back to work while I still can. And, maybe, I'll get to eat tomorrow. It was nice meeting you though, Doc. I confess succumbing to momentary self-delusion when I heard they'd brought you in. Let myself believe that you could help."

As he braced himself to stand, she found herself not wanting to see him leave. This was the longest conversation she'd had in many years. He was interesting. She was still curious about his "gift".

"Hold on," she told him. "They can make me stay here, but they don't *want* to make me stay."

He gave her a quizzical look.

"I spoke to the guy in charge. Singh, I believe. From what he said it's clear that he wants me to feel comfortable and safe. Otherwise, they could have just dragged me here at gunpoint, and would not have made a point of telling me about you. They want me to *want* to stay here. Guess it's safer if the woman holding the scalpel *likes* you rather than fears you when you need her."

He nodded, furrowed his brow. "Thinking about it," he said, "it's terrifying, the power a surgeon holds. The power to save or kill someone at their most vulnerable."

"And, for the rest of you, it'd be hard to differentiate between the calculated use of one of those powers and an earnest, but failed attempt to exercise the other."

He smiled and narrowed his eyes at her.

"Hope you're not trying to threaten me, Doc."

"Of course not," she said with a short chuckle. "Quite the opposite. I have a proposition."

"Go on."

"Look," she tapped one of the boxes on her desk, "Singh wants me to do an inventory of anything with possible medical application amongst your foodstuffs and supplies. If I find any analgesics, anything that can help with the inflammation, I'll put some aside for you."

"There you go," he said, shaking his head slightly. "Giving me false hope again."

"You're right," she admitted. "Odds aren't great that I'll find a cabinet full of aspirin that everyone here thought was rat poison. But, even if I never find anything helpful, the people who control your rations are the same people who want me comfortable here. I can make sure they know that I'm happy to stay because of you. I can even insist they keep you around after your hands are useless."

He considered her proposal and then shrugged.

"What you're saying makes a lot of sense, Doc. You can save me . . . even if you can't help me . . . Eh, what the hell, Doc. What do you want to know? Ask away."

"Well," she said. "First of all, have you spoken to . . . that Steven fella for the day?"

"About what?"

His expression was blank.

"About the devices I brought with me. Not particularly concerned whether you discussed breakfast."

There was a fleeting look of recognition in the man's eyes.

"Would have been a terribly brief discussion if we had. But, yes, I've seen them. A tiny black phone with a cracked casing, and a silver tablet with finicky touch controls."

"Oh. So you got them working."

It was strange for her to think of seeing those devices blink to life again after so many years; to think of seeing the images lost to the electronic depths beyond black screens. It was a miracle that she had held on to them this long, that she had them in her tent when the men with guns had appeared.

"*I* didn't make them work," he assured her. "That was the other guy. He's a magician with electronics, and quite the scavenger. You should see his workspace. It's a Frankenstein's monster of wires, exposed circuits, and old batteries and gadgets of every shape and size. Hell, I could show it to you later. He also maintains the generator downstairs, though we rarely use it. Precious little gas left."

"Impressive," she remarked. "Easy to see how he lasted so long. Has a skill-set critical to rebuilding, or, more realistically, clinging to some vestige of what we lost. Makes him valuable."

"Just like you, Doc."

"And, strangely enough, like you."

"Yeah, imagine that."

"You know," he said, with a heavy sigh, "when they first paired me up with him that was what it was about. Rebuilding. Well . . . actually, at first it was personal correspondence, blog posts and the like from loved ones. Whatever wasn't lost to the "cloud" on servers halfway across the world that probably don't exist anymore. But, once you're dead, no one gives a damn about a collection of emails to your dead wife. And people kept dying.

"*Then* it was about rebuilding, archiving all of the history, culture, text books, maps, schematics . . . recipes. Anything important for remembering and restoring what we lost. Anything without hardcopies. Things that would be gone for good when the printer ink dried up, the batteries all died and the gas was all burned.

"But then people accepted that survival just means a slow death. Just staving off the decay as long as possible with no hope of restoration or progress. So now I transcribe tales of fantasy and intrigue from old e-readers, so that the few of us left can try to forget how screwed we are for a few hours."

"What were you in your past life?" she asked. "I was then what I am now. But *your* current job didn't really exist back then. Were you a teacher, something where a photographic memory might be helpful?"

"Nah," he replied, drawing out the word. "There's no real connection between who I was then and what I am now. I don't dwell on that other man. He's dead and buried."

"Okay. If you don't want to talk about that. How about your partner, was he an engineer or electrician in his past life?"

The record keeper chuckled. "Our actual discussions probably tend closer to breakfast choices than the sharing of profound revelations about our past."

"You work with him, I'm guessing, almost every day, but you don't have any real conversations?"

"Those are complicated," he said dismissively. "We just stick to our process. He finds a way to power the devices long enough for me to read the content. Then I write, or typed—back when the typewriter still worked, and we could still scrounge up ribbons for it. The rest is just noise."

"And how long have the two of you been doing this? How long has this settlement been here? How did they discover your skill? Did you offer yourself up?"

He gave a dry chuckle. "Been doing this about as long as we've been here. One of those things where you just fall into a role; find a way to make yourself useful, because useful is worth keeping alive. It's basically been the same routine day-in and day-out for all those years. Time sorta just lost meaning after a while. I'm sure that you know how it is, Doc."

She had stopped trying to count the days and the years long ago. She could hardly venture a guess as to how long. But, then, she was not the one who was supposed to have a perfect memory.

"You keep calling me 'Doc'," she remarked. "But you said that you got my tablet working. My name is all over that thing. Certainly you would've seen it. And, certainly, *you* would remember it."

He hesitated.

"Of course," she continued, "as far as I recall, no one was ever proven to possess such a skill. There were several people known for remarkable memories, sure. But they used memorization techniques."

"I can certainly tell you your name, Dr. Schwimmer," he said, holding his hands in front of him as if flipping through the pages of a book, although not looking down at it. "Melissa Schwimmer. I can also tell you about your digital collection of bodice rippers and detective novels."

She realized what he was doing with his hands. He was miming swiping through the contents of a touch-screen device.

Probably a visualization technique to help him remember. He might not even be aware that he was doing it.

"I can tell you about the romantic rendezvous between Hans and Margarette on the beaches of Ibiza," he continued. "About the beach resort where they stayed at Playa d'en Bossa. About the pool there, and the concert stage across the courtyard from it, with the half-dome ceiling supporting an arch of floodlights.

"I could tell you about the peach-coloured walls of their room, with the unusual green stain that Margarette couldn't stop looking at, and about the bellhop with the styled moustache who seemed to fancy her. Or I could tell you whodunit in the case of the St. Helena murders."

"Hold off on that last one," she told him, holding up a hand. "I've long forgotten how that book ends. In case you do manage to transcribe it, I wouldn't want you to ruin the surprise."

"Well, I couldn't *really* spoil that anyway," he confessed. "Didn't get that far. I could, however, tell you detective Furlong's favourite dish at the Italian place he frequents. That came up in chapter three."

"Do you always read pieces of several things at once? Or were you just trying to sample everything my collection had to offer in the little time you had with it?"

"A little bit of both. Wanted to see what was there; maybe something I liked. But I do actually find it helpful to jump from novel to novel like that, instead of reading each all the way through."

"So, that's part of your memorization system? Are names difficult for you in general, or just mine?"

She recalled his seeming confusion when she had asked about his partner by name.

"Look, I don't really have some formalized system," he said, agitatedly. "And I stumbled on your name, because I try not to associate real names with anything."

"Real names?"

"Yeah, real people's names. I do whatever I can to not associate them with what I read, or with photographs, faces. I always try to avoid thinking about what story, what document or correspondence, what face belongs with what name. Otherwise I would start to obsess about it. And, eventually, I would ask someone something that I shouldn't."

"Like what?"

"Like, what happened to your son?"

She froze. Silent. As the barriers in her mind began to crumble, she thought of her child's smiling eyes, of his infectious laughter. It had been so long since she had seen a child. That had made it easier not to think of him.

"You're right," she finally said. "You probably shouldn't ask such things."

"Sorry," he said feebly, staring down at his hands. "The picture of you two . . . It was your tablet's background image. First thing I saw when it was turned on. The resemblance was unmistakable . . . He had your eyes."

His chuckle was completely mirthless.

"You were quite the looker back then," he said. "Smooth, caramel skin, dark, braided hair, hazel eyes, and a gorgeous smile."

"So," she said, quickly wiping away the teardrop that had been welling up in the corner of her eye. "You're saying that I'm not a looker now?"

He smiled weakly, glancing up at her sheepishly. "Time's been unkind to us all, I think. Don't know about you, but I don't spend much time in front of mirrors anymore. Don't know just how wrinkled, decrepit and scarred I've become in my advanced age."

"I already told you," she said with her own weak grin. "You look like shit . . . Remember?"

There was actual liveliness in his laugh this time.

"Oh, I've forgotten so much," he said, sighing. Then he leaned forward and whispered to her in a conspiratorial tone. "Don't tell anyone I said that. Kinda undermines the whole keep-me-around- because-I-remember-good pitch."

"I imagine that you'd have to forget a lot to keep cramming new stories into your head."

"The old stories I remember fine," he told her, solemnly. "All of the words, the details, the recipes and equations. Don't understand half of it, but I remember. Images are harder. I lose details after a while, get confused . . . Pieces that scatter in the wind."

"Excuse me?"

He looked over at the door.

"Getting back to that first question you asked me," he said. "About what my oldest memories are like . . . With images, faces . . . It's like seeing . . . like *feeling* a vague impression embossed on varnished wood. The details, the texture, the granularity has been smoothed out, just leaving an indistinct shape.

"The details come with effort. But I have to focus on a particular part of the image. Can't ever seem to hold the entire thing in my mind. The older the memory, the less of it that I can clearly visualize at once.

"It's like starting with a featureless mannequin, and having the shards of a shattered porcelain face that you're trying to piece together like a puzzle. Only you have no glue to keep the pieces together, so you're struggling to hold them all in place at once."

She noted they had returned to the violent imagery of their initial exchange. The image of a loved one's face shattered. So he had not been describing some traumatic recollection, but rather how his memory worked in general.

She was surprised that he had been so frank about that with a stranger. But, then, his response had been so off-putting it had made her drop that line of questioning. Perhaps that had been his intention.

"So maybe you can just hold together the image of the eyes," he continued. "Or maybe just a smile, or even just a hairline. What's worse is that you're not sure that all the pieces belong to the same face. You have all these scattered fragments of shattered visages swirling in the wind around you, and you don't know which ones to grab to assemble your puzzle.

"So that's what it's like for me. Piecing together bits of different faces, different images. Trying to sort out what does and doesn't belong. Am I remembering the right nose that goes with those eyes, the right door that goes with that house? Or am I mixing up two . . . *somehow* . . . similar faces, similar buildings.

"Even recent memories get jumbled sometimes. No firewall for the associations of my cluttered mind. Just a twisted mess that I'm constantly trying to untangle. But those associations continue to come unbidden."

He looked at her with wavering eyes.

"I look at your face now," he said, "as . . . *different* as it may be, and I see that picture of you with your arms wrapped around your boy. Then I remember, *years* ago, seeing a child frozen from exposure in his dead mother's embrace.

"That was in the early days. But, like the kid with the cracked skull outside, I see them every time I climb the steps of this building. Every time I tread over the memory of their corpses. That repetition keeps the image clear. Can't hold on to everything; can't choose what to forget."

She focused on that word. Repetition.

"You mentioned not wanting to obsess. Is *that* how you memorize things? Are you obsessive compulsive? It sometimes lends itself to remarkable recall."

"The others basically just think that I look at something and take a mental snapshot. The truth is a lot . . . *noisier.*"

"You repeat things to yourself in your head over and over, don't you? See the same words and images again and again?"

"It helps that I can speed read," he told her. "Words tend to repeat in the order I read them. I started to forget about more recent things before the echoes caught up. Jumping from book to book seemed to help with that. My mind can get back to things before they slip away from it.

"I try to forget the older things once I've written them down; make it easier to remember everything else. But those are the ones that have been repeated the most, the ones that are in there the deepest. It's very hard to make them stop."

"How do you even function?"

"How do *any* of us function?" he retorted. "I guess obsession is my own escape from reality. And, since it's not my own life that I'm obsessing over, I avoid painful reminders of personal loss.

"Of course, it can be overwhelming at times; all the noise in my head; voices of hundreds of different authors, letter writers, and everyone else. My private chorus of cicadas and crickets chirping in my skull, now that the real ones are gone.

"I do my best to keep to myself, avoid conversations, extra noise. Luckily, no one's particularly chatty these days."

"I don't know," she remarked. "You seem oddly talkative for someone who doesn't like conversing."

"Ever had someone call you out by name, but you can't quite place them, and don't want to say?"

She nodded. There had been some awkward social gatherings in a previous life.

"That's what I do whenever necessary. I try to ignore the noise in my head while I talk to strangers like they're old friends. Strangers who I may have known for years. Steer the conversation to what I know. Speak of the general. Dance around forgotten details. Avoid the personal. Avoid names. Think I got pretty good at it at some point."

"Were you always like this? Or was obsessiveness a coping mechanism?"

"I'm beginning to feel *studied*, Doc," he said, leaning back. "You going to start taking notes?"

"I'll admit, I was intrigued when I heard about you," she conceded. "Not much left in this world that I can say that about."

"Is there anything on that old tablet you want preserved, or was your only interest discovering whether I was truly what they said?"

She thought about her collection of half-forgotten whodunits and silly romances on the device. She thought about the desktop image, her son's smile. Her own unbidden association.

"There're a few things on there that I wouldn't mind having written out," she told him, putting Isaiah out of her mind. "But, like you, I'm not really interested in dwelling on my past."

"You planning to leave now that you know the truth about me? Might be able to help the others around here, even if I'm a lost cause."

"Have nowhere better to be. And I doubt that your friends outside, with the rifles, would just *let* me leave. Besides, we made a deal. You talked to me about your memories, so I'll impress upon your keepers the value of sustaining you."

"Honouring your word, huh?" He seemed pleasantly surprised. "Thought honesty died with civilization. Hard to trust when every little advantage means so much."

"Maybe a little easier now that everything seems to mean so little."

"Fair point," he conceded. "But even the hopeless might fight over scraps."

"How much do you remember," she asked, "of your life before the world went to hell?"

"I remember by repetition, Doc. Routine. I wake up in the same cold, dark room every morning; in the same pain. What came before the routine? Where did I wake before that room? When wasn't I in pain? That was drowned out long ago . . ."

He gazed past her at nothing in particular.

"I sometimes see a face," he almost whispered. "Parts of one anyway. I think she was someone important. Someone who made me feel safe. But her likeness slipped away. Shattered and scattered on the wind.

"The most vivid image in my mind is of an old swing set on a grassy lawn. One of the swings is broken, the wooden seat dragging on the ground, hanging limply from a single chain.

"But was it mine, something from my childhood? Or was it just a dream, or something I read in a book? That one image sticks with me, and I don't even know if it's real. Yet I can't remember the face of anyone that I loved."

"There's a cost to remembering. Would it be better to be like you, to forget the things that were lost?"

She had certainly spent much of the last few decades trying to forget.

"I can't really answer that."

"Not asking you to."

"I can only say that some people here still want my partner to let them look at the old photos on their phones every now and then. Some don't. And *I* sometimes wish I had some treasured memory to hold onto, wish I could remember what that important person looked like, who she was."

She was not sure that she could bear to look at Isaiah's face now.

"You don't even remember her name?"

"Nah."

Sad, feeble husk that he was, he had not looked as pathetic before as he did now, sitting there, staring down at the floor. No, she certainly did not want to be like him.

"And what about *your* name?" she asked. "No one mentioned it."

He looked up at her, his expression blank.

"Sometimes I wish I could remember that too."

"Sorry." She did not know what else to say.

"Don't waste your time pitying me. It doesn't make sense. And, soon enough, I won't even remember that you did. Just keep your word about advocating for me, and keep what I told you confidential–doctor-patient and all that–and I'll just go back to my routine."

"You could stop by," she suggested. "Make it part of your routine. I'd . . . forgotten what it's like to just have a conversation. It's a welcome change."

He shrugged with pronounced effort.

"Sure, Doc. Just be prepared to hear me repeat myself a lot."

"I'll try to not point it out."

"Appreciate it."

She chuckled lightly.

"What a strange friend I've made."

A smile brightened his countenance somewhat.

"Is that what we are, friends?"

"Not really sure. Been so long since I had one. But I think so."

"Not sure I remember how friendship works."

"There must be some balance," she said, feeling as if pleading with the universe. "Some way to hold onto the pleasant memories, and let go what came after."

"Think you're describing Alzheimer's, Doc–been dreading that . . . You *can* have balance; remembering good *and* bad."

"But *you* can't."

"Guess not. Also can't help you live in the past without losing your mind, just provide momentary escape into fantasy. But, if you want to talk, I'll talk. Maybe you'll tell me about your boy someday. The written word sticks in my head more easily, so you'd have to repeat yourself a lot, telling me what makes him special, what it's like to treasure pleasant memories of him. The ones that came after . . . just leave out."

"That . . . might just be wonderful," she said sincerely, images of better days flickering in her mind. "You're a good man . . . whoever you are."

"Guess I made a good impression."

"*Unforgettable.*"

He laughed with surprising volume. "Think I'll enjoy this friendship thing, Doc."

No point, she supposed, in asking him to call her Melissa.

"Think I will too."

H.K. WILLIAMS

Cascadura
Trinidad & Tobago

I t is the morning of the interview and I wake up to the smell of vomit. There on the floor, right next to my face, is a puddle of sleeping pills half melted in bile. How many did I take? I see the bottle under the bed and in reaching for it, I push it further away. Doesn't matter, they didn't work. Not that I expected them to, but it has become a habit to hope. Too tired to move, I remain propped against the bedframe. Failed suicides are exhausting.

"Syndra."

My house-bot glides into the room and greets me with her metallic staccato. "Good morning, Renae."

I really have to get her voicebox fixed.

When she sees the mess, she immediately gets down on her knees and begins cleaning, so I pull myself up onto the bed and out of her way. I have to be in the studio by noon, but the cool sheets are a welcome relief after spending the night contorted on the floor.

My handheld lies dormant on the pillow. There are no messages. Jackson hasn't replied, but the video he sent last night is cued for replay. He wants to run it before we begin the interview. One tap and an image of Jackson in soft focus projects onto the bedroom wall. His voice, weighted with gravitas, asks, "What would you do if you realised you could not die?" I mute the sound; no need for the melodrama with the memories. He fades from view and the montage silently continues with pictures from my wedding.

Richard and I in front of City Hall—he in his light-grey suit (he never liked wearing dark colours, since he figured they did not go well with his sapodilla complexion), me in a knee-length white dress. Richard smiling at the camera, me smiling at him, our friends smiling at us in the background. The picture then morphs into our first interview, a couple of weeks after we received confirmation. My features unchanged, his beard slightly salted by then. My geneticist Dr. Klein beaming at me as he explained to the world how my cells have stopped aging, refusing to die even when exposed to the most virulent diseases.

"I am cautiously optimistic," he declared. "However, I am certain that Renae holds the key to human longevity."

They never found the key in time for Richard. I see myself in the video in an old press photo at his funeral. I stop the clip and the image fades from the wall. Cancer. We never had children; it seemed that I could only retain life, not give it. Richard always said that he didn't mind, that we would be our own legacy. Even now I can never get used to the cool emptiness on the left side of the bed.

"What would you like for breakfast?"

Syndra, finished with the cleaning, displays today's menu from her hand.

"Just coffee. Thanks."

Strong and black. Of course, now it is made from synthetic beans, but after all these years mankind has not found a better drink. Maybe I can say that in the interview. She returns with the steaming mug, which I take to the window. It is raining below. Lightning blossoms through the dark grey clouds hundreds of feet below. On days like these I am grateful to have a rent-controlled apartment above the weather. Those living on the lower levels will have to activate their rain shields. But even that is better than living in the inner core of a sky-tower. There, one is engulfed by the dimly lit darkness, which is punctuated by the noise and lights from the sky trains.

"Any messages, Syndra?"

"There are no new messages."

I am starting to feel anxious. Why hasn't he sent over the question list?

"Would you like me to put you through to the studio?"

"No, never mind; bring my closet."

She joins me at the window and displays a holographic image of my closet; selecting a long-sleeved navy-blue dress for my approval.

"It's slimming, and covers your scars."

She knows I'm self-conscious about the two keloid scars which formed after I slit my wrists. I am sure Jackson will bring it up; and the media circus that followed. He will lean in, probably even hold my hand, and say something like: "I know it must have been hard for you, knowing that your husband and loved ones have passed on, leaving you behind."

Camera two will zoom in for a close-up, anticipating tears.

"Is that why you tried to take your own life? Did you ever try again?"

My life is now entertainment. I only agreed to do this for the Bitcoin. Longevity is expensive.

"Your taxi will be here in exactly seventeen and a half minutes," Syndra announces.

"Bring me another cup of coffee."

"You will be late," she counters.

"They'll wait."

As the world's oldest living human, all I have is time.

* * *

"Take me to Sky Tower Ten in the Metropolitan quadrant, level 187."

An hour later and I am making my way through the inter-tower highway to Aexus Studios. Usually I take the sky trains when I need to go out, but not today. My face appears in the 3D Holo-ads promoting tonight's interview, so I'll be easily recognised.

Hovercycles dart in and out of the traffic. People stand along the moving pavements on their way to back to work from lunch. Most stare ahead blankly as they drift through the countless ads popping up in their path. It really isn't that much different from when I came to New York over two centuries ago. Back then it was said that you could always pick out a stranger in New York City. Tourists looked up. New Yorkers looked ahead.

Winter was early that year, and I was not prepared. The boots I salvaged from the Goodwill were too loose around my ankles, so snow kept getting in. I needed a job. My options, even with a bachelor's degree, were taking care of either an elderly person or a baby. One way or the other, it would involve diapers.

"Why you sounding so?" was always the first question my mother asked when I called home, "When you coming back?" the last. I couldn't tell her the truth: that I was lonely and earning much less than I had anticipated. The Rosens—the couple who eventually hired me to care for their twin girls—were nice enough, but they both worked long hours in Manhattan, so I hardly saw them.

"When you coming back?"

"I just need to save a little more money."

"When you coming back?"

"As soon as the girls finish school."

She had stopped asking after I had stayed away for three years.

My face pops up in front of me. I'd forgotten to ask the driver to turn off the Holo-ads. Here I am, smiling, cheek to cheek with talk-show host Jackson Ross.

"Join me tonight for my exclusive one-on-one with Renae Celestine, the world's oldest living human. Find out what life was like before the Shifts. Does she hold the key to our survival as a species? Tune in on . . ."

"Can you turn off the ads, please?"

"Sure, no problem. So what do you think about that Renae woman? You're going to the studio, right? You work there?"

I keep silent, avoiding his eyes as he glances at me through the rear-view mirror.

"I tried to get a ticket for the studio audience, but I wasn't picked. I'm really into history, so I wanted to meet her, you know."

I toy with the idea of introducing myself just to see his reaction, but he continues: "Imagine, she lived outside. I mean, now they're saying that the gases are decreasing, but that might take years, you know, centuries, even before we can live outside. I mean, two hundred and seventy-five years! Can you imagine? Most of us are lucky to pass fifty. I wonder if they will ever figure out what is so special about her DNA. It might be too late for us, but the next generation, or maybe the one after that, could live forever."

I glimpse his face through the rear-view mirror and notice the crow's feet at his eyes and the deep creases bracketing his mouth. He cannot be less than thirty. More than half his life gone. He dyed his hair green, and it clashes with his caramel-coloured skin.

"Don't you think she probably suffered through enough experiments—and for what? They still aren't any closer to figuring it out. They say her survival is a mystery. For all we know, she might be just as fed up of living as you are of watching people die."

"Nah, nobody wants to die," he counters with a grin. "Besides, she witnessed everything. It must have been so exciting . . ."

"Exciting? Exciting, you say. The earthquakes, feeling like the entire planet was falling apart. Billions dying. I thought everyone was going to die, I thought I was going to be the only one left . . ."

I stop talking, realising that we have stopped moving. My outburst seems to echo in the cab.

"I can't believe it's actually you . . . I didn't mean to . . . I'm sorry . . . I didn't realise . . ."

I stop him before he can utter any more incomplete sentences.

"It's fine. Can we go? I'm already late as it is."

"Yeah, sure, sure."

And after he fumbles with the ignition, we continue on our way. How am I going to handle this interview, if a few questions from a cab driver can upset me like that?

"Excuse me, but can I ask you something?"

"Sure."

"Were giraffes really that tall? Did you ever see one? They said New York had one of the best zoos in the world. Were their necks really that long?"

"What's your name?"

"Sebastien."

I decide to tell him what he needs to hear.

"Yes, Sebastien, they really were that tall. Life was really great back then. We didn't know how good we had it."

A satisfied smile spreads across his face and we continue to the studio in silence.

"I am sorry, Ms. Celestine, but Mr. Ross is in a meeting right now. Maybe . . ."

"Look, just tell Jackson that he can interview himself if he doesn't come and explain this."

I press the remote and the door to my dressing room slides

shut. The production assistant has just dropped off the interview questions, and the first question is a surprise. It is about Trinidad. Jackson did his homework.

I am not prepared to talk about that. What can I say? It was so long ago. That we should have recognised the signs? They used to say that "God is a Trini." So it made sense that he would warn his children first.

I remember watching the young East Indian fisherman as he related his discovery to the news camera. Bare-backed children hovered around him, grinning, as he revelled in his sudden importance. How he was late that morning. How he was walking through the track to the beach and all he was studying was where he would find the money to get a new engine for the boat and schoolbooks for the children. How he did not notice anything until he stepped on one, and when he saw it was a hummingbird, he crossed himself. Don't mind he wasn't a Christian, but everybody know that the hummingbird sacred and he didn't want no bad luck to follow him out to sea, especially with all them Venezuelan pirates around. How is only when he reach the beach he realise what was going on.

The camera then followed his outstretched arm. Littered on the shore were hundreds of little bodies, wings splayed as if crucified, each one a bejewelled canopic jar laid out on an altar of sand. Waves weeping at the feet of those nearest the water.

Strange thing, memory: the things it allows you to forget. I can still see that scene so clearly, yet I cannot remember my mother's face. But I do remember her voice; the sing-song accent, which left this world centuries ago; and her scent—garlic. She constantly drank garlic tea for her pressure. It was especially high when I told her that I was leaving for the States. I was twenty-seven at the time, and her only child.

"America! You don't watch news? What you want to go live in that ketch-ass place for? I mad call the embassy and tell them to deport your ass as soon as you land in JFK."

But I had already quit my job as a receptionist at the Hilton, lied on my visa application, and converted my entire savings to US dollars, so there was no turning back. Besides, it was only to be for a year, just until I saved enough to put my business degree to use and start my own company.

"I don't see why you can't take your time and save your money here. But no, allyuh must have everything one time. After how I sacrifice and send you to school, you going up there to be a maid. Eh, is that what you go do your poor mother, girl?"

She stopped speaking to me, and for the weeks leading up to my departure I endured cut-eyes and sighs every time I entered the house. Then one day she surprised me by cooking curried cascadura and rice.

"To make sure you come back," she explained.

"I will come back, I promise. I don't need no fish to bring me back," I replied, touched by the gesture. "Besides," I continued through the forkfuls, careful to avoid the tiny bones, "you know that legend not true."

"You don't know that. Once you eat the fish you bound to end your days here. Everybody I know who eat it and went away come back and dead right here. It real scarce these days, but I was able to get some."

I remember asking her why she didn't eat.

"No, I don't want none. I ain't going nowhere. Make sure and eat all."

I did, and though my memories have faded, I always remember that she smiled as she cleared my empty plate.

The production assistant returns without Jackson.

"Mr. Ross is really sorry, but he's still tied up in meetings. But he did say to tell you that he would make some time to chat with you a few minutes before the show."

Tied up in meetings. Yeah, right, he's probably getting his beard dyed.

He continues through my silence.

"This is Misha. She will be doing your hair and makeup," he says, introducing the woman at his side. "And I see you've brought your own outfit." He gestures to my dress, which I've laid out on the sofa. He doesn't seem impressed by my selection.

"If you feel like wearing something else, please feel free to let me know. We have several options available in all the latest styles."

"Thanks, I'll bear that in mind."

He continues when he realises that I have refused to take his hint. "So, I will be back in one hour to take you to the set."

I am now alone with Misha, who has been openly staring at me throughout the exchange. She is dressed in black and sports a steel-grey mohawk with several tribal designs shaved onto both sides of her head. I can't tell how old she is. Her face is unlined and dewy looking. It could be the makeup, or it could be youth. I'm leaning towards it being the makeup.

"Well, I guess we should get started."

She nods and begins to take out her tools from her metal case. As I settle into the chair by the mirror I am surprised to see brushes, liquid foundation, eyeshadow, blushes and the like emerge.

"You do makeup the old-fashioned way?"

"Yes, I specialise in vintage beauty trends. I thought you would feel more comfortable that way."

"Oh." I am touched by her consideration.

"There is just one small problem."

"What's that?"

"I don't have your shade. I've never met anyone with your complexion. It's such a rich warm brown, like chocolate. I can mix something . . ."

She trails off when she sees my expression in the mirror. She's right, no one has my shade any more. Those who survived were forced to live together, and as a result ethnicities are now blurred to the point where everyone—she, Sebastian, Jackson, everyone—is the same shade of caramel brown. She looks at me with a mixture of helplessness and pity. It is the same look that Mrs. Rosen gave me the day it happened. The day I stopped aging. October 3rd, 2021.

I had just returned home from dropping the twins to school. The phone rang and my friend Althea, who looked after Mr. Charles in the neighbouring apartment, was screaming for me to turn on the TV to CNN. I was afraid that it was a terrorist attack, since I was set to return home in a few days. My mother was ill. After seven years in the US, it was time to go back.

When I turned on the TV the images were worse. The view overlooking the Caribbean Sea showed thousands of corpses like little atolls floating on the waves. I tried to make sense of the images by reading the ticker at the bottom of the screen. A series of catastrophic earthquakes had destroyed my island home. It was the first of the Igneous Shifts. Confused, I reached for the phone and dialled my mother's number. Just last week she had told me about all the tremors the island was experiencing. The terse recording, "Your correspondent is not reachable," made the reality of what had happened clear. My mother was gone, my home, my country, everything was gone.

That was how Mrs. Rosen found me, sitting quietly on the floor with the phone in my hand. She stormed into the apartment, upset that she had had to leave Midtown during rush hour because I had forgotten to pick up the girls. When she finally understood what had happened, the four of us sat watching the TV, listening to the experts talk about subduction zones and seismic shifts. And there we remained until she gave me a Valium and took me to bed, all the while berating herself for forgetting that

Trinidad was my homeland when she had first come across the story on her Twitter feed earlier that day.

Eventually I became a US citizen. I was an "undocumented immigrant", but my landless state meant there was nowhere for me to be deported to. I believe that the same applies to my existence. No island to return to, nowhere to end my days. I am left here to linger. The scientists can keep looking for answers; but I know the truth. How else can I explain the agelessness, the failed suicide attempts? I don't call this living; that ended years ago.

"Are you ok? I didn't mean to make you cry."

I try to compose myself, as I only have twenty minutes left before I have to be on set.

"No, it's fine. Come, make me pretty."

"Prettier," Misha quips as she blends the makeup into the tracks left by my tears.

Syndra is waiting for me when I get home. She starts relating all the messages she received whilst I was out. I put her on silent mode. I'm not in the mood, even though the interview was a success. I peel off the red pantsuit I wore for the show; Misha had convinced me to wear it and I have to admit that I looked really good. Jackson was pleased, the studio was pleased, and my bank account will be pleased by tomorrow morning.

I make my way to the bathroom. There, perched on the edge of the tub, I watch the water quickly make its way up from my ankles to my calves, then I slide underneath. This feels good. If I keep my eyes closed, even in this cramped space, I can summon a favourite memory.

After a two-hour hike, we arrived at a river somewhere in Valencia. It was so quiet that you could hear the bamboo bending with the breeze. I remember the smooth firmness of the river stones as I waded in, the crisp, cold water and the way the sunlight warmed my skin in patches as it poked through the leaves.

I stay lying on the floor of the tub until the water gets cold. My chest never tightens; there is no need for air. My body flows through death, like a cascadura in a stream. I release a sigh and watch it bubble to the surface. Then, gripping the sides, I pull myself up, step out of the tub and leave a trail of wet footprints all the way to my bed.

About the Contributors

Ararimeh Aiyejina is a Nigerian-born citizen of Trinidad and Tobago, who graduated with a BSE in Chemical Engineering from Princeton University in 2009, and who is currently pursuing a postgraduate degree at the St. Augustine Campus of the University of the West Indies. While an undergraduate at Princeton, he enrolled in creative writing courses and was awarded the Outstanding Sophomore Award in Creative Writing in 2007.

Tammi Browne-Bannister was born in Antigua and lives in Barbados. She learned everything about writing from The Barbados Community College under the capable hands of Canadian-Barbadian writer, editor and writing competition judge, Robert Edison Sandiford. She attended the Cropper Foundation's 8th Residential Creative Writers Workshop in Trinidad. She cares for the environment except when she goes shell hunting. Shells are her diamonds. She only pilfers those uninhabited. She buries Moon Jellyfish found dead on the sand and is happy when she finds a silver dollar. She loves sea grapes but runs away from fat porks.

Summer Edward was born and raised in Trinidad. Her work has been published in a number of periodicals including *The Missing Slate, Bim: Arts for the 21st Century, Matatu: Journal for African Culture and Society, sx salon, The Columbia Review, The Caribbean Writer, Obsidian: Literature in the African Diaspora* and others. She was shortlisted for the Small Axe Literary Prize, nominated for the Pushcart Prize, and was one of the "Who's Next?" emerging writers at the NGC Bocas Lit Fest. She lived in the United States for a decade and now divides her time between Philadelphia and Trinidad.

Brian Franklin is a Barbadian systems developer in the financial industry. He has been writing creatively since he learned how to hold a pencil. He is an avid cricket fan and lover of videogames. He maintains a website where he shares free and experimental stories, media reviews, and rants, at *Antisungrey.com*. His works draw inspiration from the societies, history and mythologies of the Caribbean region. He is a graduate of the 2014 Callaloo Barbados Creative Writing Workshop. His speculative fiction novel, *Iridium*, was shortlisted for the 2012 Frank Collymore Literary Award.

Kevin Jared Hosein currently resides in Trinidad and Tobago. He is the 2015 Caribbean regional winner of the Commonwealth Short Story Prize for his entry, "The King of Settlement 4". His first book, *Littletown Secrets*, was published in 2013. He is also featured in anthologies such as *Pepperpot: Best New Stories from the Caribbean* and *Jewels of the Caribbean*. He was shortlisted twice for the Small Axe Prize, and for the 2013 Caribbean Short Story Prize. His novel, *The Repenters*, is to be published by Peepal Tree Press in 2016.

Elizabeth J. Jones, formerly a lecturer in English at the Bermuda College, has for many years been a freelance writer, editor and tutor. She enjoys writing for magazines about all aspects of Bermuda, including its wildlife, history, businesses, culture and people. She has benefited enormously from attending writing workshops organised by the Bermuda Government's Department of Community Affairs and Cultural Affairs and has written several short stories, as well as a novel, all set in Bermuda.

Karen Lord a Barbadian author and research consultant, is known for her debut novel *Redemption in Indigo*, which won the

2008 Frank Collymore Literary Award, the 2010 Carl Brandon Parallax Award, the 2011 William L. Crawford Award, the 2011 Mythopoeic Fantasy Award for Adult Literature and the 2012 Kitschies Golden Tentacle (Best Debut), and was longlisted for the 2011 Bocas Prize for Caribbean Literature and nominated for the 2011 World Fantasy Award for Best Novel. Her second novel *The Best of All Possible Worlds* won the 2009 Frank Collymore Literary Award, the 2013 RT Book Reviews Reviewers' Choice Awards for Best Science Fiction Novel, and was a finalist for the 2014 Locus Awards. Its sequel, *The Galaxy Game*, was published in January 2015.

Richard B. Lynch writes in many genres, ranging from poetry to screenwriting. He works in the video and film field in his country of birth, Barbados, where he has won awards for his direction and conceptualization of music videos, and lends a hand where he can in many aspects of filmmaking. A version of this story first appeared in *POUi: Cave Hill Journal of Creative Writing*, published by the University of the West Indies.

Brandon O'Brien is a performance poet and writer from Trinidad. He has been shortlisted for the 2014 Alice Yard Prize for Art Writing and the 2014 and 2015 Small Axe Literary Competitions. He has also represented his country as a member of Trinidad and Tobago's first Brave New Voices slam team in 2008. He performs regularly with the 2 Cents Movement, is a performer and facilitator with the.art.IS Performing Arts Company, and is a recording performer on the Free Speech Project radio programme on several local radio stations across the island.

Portia Subran is an artist and writer of Trinidad and Tobago. Subran finds inspiration from her life experiences, as well as the tales of her parents. Her artwork has been featured in *Arc Magazine*, and has been shown at the Art Society of Trinidad and Tobago end of year exhibitions. In 2013, she was announced the winner of the Potbake Productions 2011-2013 Caribbean Short Story Competition with her work, "Unclipped Wings". This work was later published in the Caribbean short story collection *Jewels of the Caribbean*.

H.K. Williams is a writer from Trinidad and Tobago. In 2014 she was mentored by Earl Lovelace as an apprentice in the Mentoring with the Masters Programme, which was facilitated by the Government of Trinidad and Tobago. After successfully completing the programme she was invited to join Monique Roffey's writers' lab in Belmont, where she is currently working on producing a collection of short stories. Her work was featured in *Voicing our Vision*, a short-story anthology published by the Writers Union of Trinidad and Tobago in 2013.

Damion Wilson is a software developer, martial artist, and former bicycle racer, living and working in sunny (mostly) Bermuda. Now accompanied by a wonderful wife and two beautiful daughters, he writes using themes gleaned from the world of technology, from experiences teased from the lives of those who've touched him, and from his own life.

CPSIA information can be obtained
at www.ICGtesting.com
Printed in the USA
LVOW11s0910291116
514914LV00002B/18/P